Buchman has catapulted his way to the top tier of my favorite authors.

— FRESH FICTION

One of our favorite authors.

— RT BOOK REVIEWS

Buchman has catapulted his way to the top tier of my favorite authors.

— FRESH FICTION

A favorite author of mine. I'll read anything that carries his name, no questions asked. Meet your new favorite author!

— THE SASSY BOOKSTER, FLASH OF FIRE

M.L. Buchman is guaranteed to get me lost in a good story.

— THE READING CAFE, WAY OF THE WARRIOR: NSDQ

I love Buchman's writing. His vivid descriptions bring everything to life in an unforgettable way.

— PURE JONEL, HOT POINT

Nonstop action that will keep readers on the edge of their seats.

— *TAKE OVER AT MIDNIGHT,* LIBRARY JOURNAL

M L. Buchman's ability to keep the reader right in the middle of the action is amazing.

— LONG AND SHORT REVIEWS

The only thing you'll ask yourself is, "When does the next one come out?"

— *WAIT UNTIL MIDNIGHT,* RT REVIEWS, 4 STARS

The first…of (a) stellar, long-running (military) romantic suspense series.

— *THE NIGHT IS MINE,* BOOKLIST, "THE 20 BEST ROMANTIC SUSPENSE NOVELS: MODERN MASTERPIECES"

I knew the books would be good, but I didn't realize how good.

— NIGHT STALKERS SERIES, KIRKUS REVIEWS

Buchman mixes adrenalin-spiking battles and brusque military jargon with a sensitive approach.

— PUBLISHERS WEEKLY

13 times "Top Pick of the Month"

— NIGHT OWL REVIEWS

Tom Clancy fans open to a strong female lead will clamor for more.

— DRONE, PUBLISHERS WEEKLY

(Miranda Chase is) one of the most compelling, addicting, fascinating characters in any genre since the *Monk* television series.

— DRONE, ERNEST DEMPSEY, AUTHOR OF THE SEAN WYATT THRILLERS

(*Drone* is) the best military thriller I've read in a very long time. Love the female characters.

Superb!

A fabulous soaring thriller.

Meticulously researched, hard-hitting, and suspenseful.

Expert technical details abound, as do realistic military missions with superb imagery that will have readers feeling as if they are right there in the midst and on the edges of their seats.

THE COMPLETE HENDERSON'S RANCH STORIES

A MONTANA BIG SKY ROMANCE STORY COLLECTION

M. L. BUCHMAN

Buchman Bookworks

Receive a free book and discover more by this author at:
www.mlbuchman.com

Cover images:

Couple of cowboys with horse at sunset © adrenaline

Cowboy Couple © DMBONDARUK

- *Christmas at Henderson's Ranch* – originally published 2015
- *Reaching Out at Henderson's Ranch* – originally published 2016
- *Welcome at Henderson's Ranch* – originally published 2017
- *Finding Henderson's Ranch* – originally published 2017
- *Emily's Christmas Gift* – originally published 2018

DON'T MISS A THING!

Other works by M. L. Buchman: (* - also in audio)

Action-Adventure Thrillers

Dead Chef
One Chef!
Two Chef!

Miranda Chase
Drone*
Thunderbolt*
Condor*
Ghostrider*
Raider*
Chinook*
Havoc*
White Top*
Start the Chase*

Science Fiction / Fantasy

Deities Anonymous
Cookbook from Hell: Reheated
Saviors 101

Single Titles
Monk's Maze
the Me and Elsie Chronicles

Contemporary Romance

Eagle Cove
Return to Eagle Cove
Recipe for Eagle Cove
Longing for Eagle Cove
Keepsake for Eagle Cove

Love Abroad
Heart of the Cotswolds: England
Path of Love: Cinque Terre, Italy

Where Dreams
Where Dreams are Born
Where Dreams Reside
Where Dreams Are of Christmas*
Where Dreams Unfold
Where Dreams Are Written
Where Dreams Continue

Non-Fiction

Strategies for Success
Managing Your Inner Artist/Writer
Estate Planning for Authors*
Character Voice
Narrate and Record Your Own
Audiobook*

Short Story Series by M. L. Buchman:

Action-Adventure Thrillers

Dead Chef

Miranda Chase Origin Stories

Romantic Suspense

Antarctic Ice Fliers

US Coast Guard

Contemporary Romance

Eagle Cove

Other

Deities Anonymous (fantasy)

Single Titles

The Emily Beale Universe
(military romantic suspense)

The Night Stalkers
MAIN FLIGHT
The Night Is Mine
I Own the Dawn
Wait Until Dark
Take Over at Midnight
Light Up the Night
Bring On the Dusk
By Break of Day
Target of the Heart
Target Lock on Love
Target of Mine
Target of One's Own
NIGHT STALKER HOLIDAYS
*Daniel's Christmas**
*Frank's Independence Day**
*Peter's Christmas**
Christmas at Steel Beach
*Zachary's Christmas**
*Roy's Independence Day**
*Damien's Christmas**
Christmas at Peleliu Cove

Henderson's Ranch
*Nathan's Big Sky**
*Big Sky, Loyal Heart**
*Big Sky Dog Whisperer**
*Tales of Henderson's Ranch**

Shadow Force: Psi
*At the Slightest Sound**
*At the Quietest Word**
*At the Merest Glance**
*At the Clearest Sensation**

Dilya's Dog Force
(formerly:
White House Protection Force)
*Off the Leash**
*On Your Mark**
*In the Weeds**

Firehawks
Pure Heat
Full Blaze
*Hot Point**
*Flash of Fire**
Wild Fire
SMOKEJUMPERS
*Wildfire at Dawn**
*Wildfire at Larch Creek**
*Wildfire on the Skagit**

Delta Force
*Target Engaged**
*Heart Strike**
*Wild Justice**
*Midnight Trust**

Emily Beale Universe Short Story Series
The Night Stalkers
The Night Stalkers Stories
The Night Stalkers CSAR
The Night Stalkers Wedding Stories
The Future Night Stalkers

Delta Force
Th Delta Force Shooters
The Delta Force Warriors

Firehawks
The Firehawks Lookouts
The Firehawks Hotshots
The Firebirds

Dilya's Dog Force
Stories

Future Night Stalkers
Stories (Science Fiction)

The Emily Beale Universe
Reading Order Road Map

any series and any novel may be read stand-alone
(all have a complete heartwarming happy ever after)

* *Formerly*: White House Protection Force
For more information and alternate reading orders, please visit:
www.mlbuchman.com/reading-order

CONTENTS

RANCH CHRONOLOGY

FIVE STORIES OF THE ORIGINS, LIVES, AND LOVES AT HENDERSON'S RANCH (AND WHERE THE 3 NOVELS FIT BEST).

*N*ote: *all stories are complete and stand-alone. They may be read in any order. But background characters do reappear. So this is a "best" order but not required at all.*

• *Christmas at Henderson's Ranch* – She flew in to work as a nanny for the owners, but her heart never let her leave.

• *Reaching Out at Henderson's Ranch* – The PTSD threatens to finish what the explosion began, until this wounded vet meets the dog who gives him back his heart.

• *Nathan's Big Sky* (novel) – Fits here.

• *Welcome at Henderson's Ranch* – She came to write a magazine puff piece about the ranch, not knowing life could be so real.

• *Big Sky, Loyal Heart* (novel) – Fits here.

• *Finding Henderson's Ranch* – Mac and Ama find a true home.

• *Emily's Christmas Gift* – Leaving a life as a top helicopter pilot to become a mom catches up with Emily Beale, until a Christmas phone call reveals her dreams.

• *Big Sky Dog Whisperer* (novel) – Fits here.

All stories previously published separately.

INTRODUCTION

Welcome to my world of Henderson's Ranch stories.

Unlike most of my series, I'm unsure how this one came about.

In my first Night Stalkers book, *The Night Is Mine,* there is an almost throwaway line in which then-Captain Emily Beale discovers that her commander, Major Mark Henderson, flies with a photo of his family tucked into the dashboard of his Black Hawk helicopter (in Chapter 2 if you want to go looking).

Seven years later—Emily and Mark have since married, reproduced, left the military, and taken to flying firefighting helicopters (while launching multiple other book and story series). Anyway, seven years on, I was fishing around for a Christmas story to tell. Some strange corner of my writer's brain unearthed that one reference to Mark's family ranch. And I had a sudden desire to see what their Montana Ranch Christmas with the parents might look like.

M. L. BUCHMAN

Christmas and I always had a dicey relationship.

As a kid, every Christmas was spent flying from New York to Florida to see my father's parents. Coming from the snow belt to Florida meant my sister and I ran around in shorts and t-shirts in the *chilly* Florida winters and caught desperate colds every single time. But it also meant seeing my grandfather, who was *amazing.* (It wasn't until years later that I understood he and Grandma had been crap parents, which explains a lot about my father, but to us grandkids Pop Sam was *amazing.*) A major blow, he died when I was eight and the trips to Florida stopped.

Of course, my father's parents made him completely nuts, so there was a massive shadow over the season both before and after that pivotal change. My mother wanted the whole show: massive tree, caroling, bountiful presents... Let's just say that Christmas was never a comfortable season in my early life.

Years later, my two closest friends slowly brought me back to Christmas. At first we exchanged gifts in the driveway, but after a few years, we'd cook together, and eventually did a *Christmas for the Stuck* that were feasts for a dozen or more who couldn't, or didn't want to, make it home for Christmas.

It was my wife and young stepdaughter who taught me what Christmas was really about, the love and joy of simply celebrating the season—even in the meager years, the joy was huge.

This is all a long way of saying that sending Emily and Mark home for Christmas to his *parents* was a major challenge as a writer. And I can tell you that, as a writer, I look for that emotional grist, that hard story that has to be dug out and faced.

Of course, I was never expecting Chelsea to show up and take over to set the tone of an entire five-story and three-book series that was supposed to be a single Christmas tale.

CHRISTMAS AT HENDERSON'S RANCH

When on a Christmas trip to visit Mark Henderson's ranch, what appears under the tree can change your life.

Chelsea Bridges' first trip to Montana lands her at Mark Henderson and Emily Beale's family ranch. In the past she pursued adventure from hiking the Continental Divide Trail to trekking in Nepal, but this horse ranch provides a whole new world of wonders.

Doug Daniels spent three tours in the Navy before he became foreman at the ranch. He has finally found his home.

Nothing prepares them for the presents that await during Christmas at Henderson's Ranch.

The opening of this story is the arrival of Emily, Mark, and their young daughter at his family's Montana ranch.

But then Chelsea stepped off the plane.

She was born from the fact that with Mark flying as an Incident Commander – Air over forest fires, he needed a flying nanny to mind his kid. She was never named or even mentioned (until I inserted a few lines during a recent revision), but in my mind she was there, playing with the kid in the back of the plane while Mark commanded the firefight.

Like Dilya all the way back in Night Stalkers #2, *I Own the Dawn,* I never saw her coming.

Chelsea attacks life with an unabashed optimism and joy that I *try* to bring to my everyday life. She doesn't have to try, she lives that attitude in every moment, with every breath. Curiously, I never found her dark side. She simply *is* that person, all the way down to her bones. She was a joy to write in this story and in the subsequent tales.

CHAPTER 1

"*This isn't right!*"

Chelsea Bridges leaned forward to see what Emily Beale was looking at. Chelsea didn't see a thing wrong, but then she'd never been to central Montana before. Out the small plane's front windshield were miles and miles of rolling green prairie. Streams crisscrossed the grassland in a bewildering maze. The backdrop was the foothills of the Rockies breaking the skyline with their snowy peaks and conifer-clad sides. The westering sun silhouetted the hills, but lit their tops with gold.

"It's absolutely gorgeous!" Then she clamped her mouth closed. She was trying to reel it in. Emily was always so even-keeled and understated that Chelsea was constantly stumbling to be less…Chelsea. Emily was this perfect woman with a drop-dead handsome husband and about the cutest kid on the planet. Chelsea had only been their daughter's nanny for a few months, but she'd seen the deference and respect that everyone at Mount Hood Aviation's firefighter airbase paid Emily. In return, the woman was kind, courteous, and utterly terrifying. Chelsea wouldn't mind being all of those things.

Her husband Mark, who sat up front in the other pilot seat of the small plane, wasn't much more effusive—except around his daughter. At least he had a sense of humor, though not as much a one as he thought he did; an observation Chelsea kept carefully to herself.

Chelsea looked over at Tessa who was strapped in beside her. She had her tiny version of her mother's elegant nose pressed up against the window. "Green," she announced. Out her window was nothing but the rolling grasslands of eastern Montana.

"It's wrong," Mark agreed solemnly but turned enough to wink at Chelsea, or at least she presumed that's what his cheek twitch was indicating at the lower edge of his mirrored Ray-Bans. "Not much snow in the hills. Means another drought year next summer."

"That's not the problem," Emily responded. "Okay, drought is a problem. But that's not the real problem."

"What is, Emma?" Again the sassy wink that said he already knew what his wife was talking about. It was amazing that the man had survived this long. Chelsea would never dare tease Emily Beale; she could probably kill with a glance if she ever took off her own mirrored shades.

"It's December," Emily took one hand off the plane's wheel—if she was on board, she was the one doing the flying—and waved it helplessly at the stunning scenery before them. "We came to Montana for a white Christmas."

"I thought it was to see Mom and Dad."

"It's still supposed to be white," she grumbled and set up to land the plane. It was as much emotion Chelsea had seen in her entire two months with them. Emily Beale was never unkind, but she was cold. Or at least chilly. But that wasn't right either. The woman was frank and forthright, as much with her daughter as with her husband. Yet Tessa was often in her lap, welcome not as child to adult, but rather as a piece of Emily that was simply back in the place where it belonged. The mother and daughter weren't close; they were simply one when they were together. It was about the most incredible thing Chelsea had ever seen. It made her ache for a family of her own; not a familiar feeling.

Again Chelsea strained up against her seatbelt to look down. A herd of horses startled and looked up at them as they passed by. They didn't scatter and run, but they eyed the low-flying plane carefully.

"Horsies!" Tessa declared delightedly when Emily shifted her flightpath so that the herd was visible outside her daughter's window. Not cold at all, just…inscrutable.

"Yes," Chelsea encouraged the toddler. "Those are horses. Aren't they pretty?"

"Pretty!" Tessa burbled, and they laughed together with delight.

Chelsea had never seen a whole herd of horses before. There were at least fifty in the group of every shade imaginable: grays, browns, whites, blacks, and mixes in patchworks, dapples, and who knew what all. They were gone behind the plane too fast to distinguish more. She tucked away the trail mix snack they'd been sharing to make sure Tessa's blood sugar was up.

Even after two months, Chelsea wasn't quite sure how she'd ended up in this situation. Not that she was complaining, Emily and Mark were great parents and it showed in their total sweetheart of a daughter. And flying with Mark over forest fires was often very dramatic.

It had started with Aunt Betsy who was a cook for the Mount Hood Aviation helicopter and smoke jumping firefighters. When Chelsea's degree in psychology hadn't led to any kind of a useful job, her aunt had asked if she liked to fly. She'd shrugged a yes because she'd flown in passenger jets any number of times to visit grandparents, and a trip to Nepal for a backpacking gap year.

She'd now spent most of the last two months sitting in tiny planes of six or eight narrow seats and been paid to enjoy the scenery and play with a baby girl. Best job she'd ever had by a long way.

Tessa was a fixture in Mark Henderson's plane when he was flying as the Incident Commander high above the fire. What was surprising wasn't that they'd added a nanny, but rather how he'd done the job for so long without one. Tessa was a pretty low maintenance kid, but she was also eighteen months old and quite intelligent.

It was a late fire season, Mark had said, and MHA had still been flying fire in the Southwest. But, finally released from the summer contract, they'd come north for a vacation and brought Chelsea along with them. She sure as hell wasn't going home. They'd known that.

As they flew closer to the ranch, more and more fences became visible, cutting the prairie into smaller pastures and training rings. There were several barns, smaller residences, and cabins surrounding the main residence.

Emily flew once over the grand log-built ranch house and waggled the plane's wings in a friendly wave.

Chelsea pointed to out to Tessa, "Isn't it amazabiling?"

"'mazbling!" Tessa called out happily. Emily sighed audibly as she circled wide of the barn.

Chelsea wondered if Mark's habits were rubbing off on her, but she couldn't resist messing with Tessa's rapidly developing language set. They landed on a gravel strip that ended close beside the house and a large outbuilding that turned out to be a hangar.

A big man strolled out to meet them, still buttoning up his sheepskin jacket. He was an older version of Mark; just as tall, just as broad-shouldered, his light hair going silver. But Mark's face was different. Darker, broader, and his hair was thick, straight, and almost midnight black, sharing only his father's gray eyes.

The clouds of mist puffing about with each breath of Mark Senior—Mac, she reminded herself, they'd said he liked to be called Mac—had Chelsea bundling up Tessa before the plane came to a halt in front of a hangar. The ground might be snow free, but it was far colder here than Oregon where they'd boarded the plane.

CHAPTER 2

Doug Daniels had stuck his head out of the barn when he heard the plane come over low. The trademark gloss-black-and-red-flame paint job told him who was aboard. Some part of him had been alarmed that a client was in-bound for a ranch vacation even though they hadn't taken any Christmas reservations this year. But it was just Mark and his knock-out wife. He liked Mark fine, but he had trouble speaking around Emily Beale. It wasn't just the beauty, he knew how to talk to pretty women just fine; it was the fierce level of competence that she demonstrated at every turn.

He finished helping Logan pitch the hay into the stalls' feedboxes before heading out to greet them. The air had a sharp bite to it, wholly different from the horse-and-straw of the barn, but no moisture. As he stepped out of the barn, he noticed that there wasn't even a hint of cloud in the cobalt blue of the late afternoon sky. The temperature was already dropping though it was still an hour to sunset. It was going to get cold tonight.

Doug stuck his head back inside. "Hey, Logan. Open up the gates. If the main herd has any sense, they'll be coming this way by sunset."

"You bet, boss. Any horse that stays out there tonight needs his horse-sense meter checked."

Doug went out to help stow the plane. There was room in the hangar because he'd moved the helicopter tight to the side after the morning's flight to check the main herd and make sure there were no stray or injured. He hadn't been able to get an accurate count, but it had felt low and that was bothering him. Happened all the time. Still, it worried him.

He ducked through the hangar's side door, popped the release, and slid open the main door from the inside. It rattled and boomed in the cold air. A sharp squeal in one of the wheels had him adding "needs grease" to the infinite mental checklist that was running a working dude ranch.

Just emerging from the plane was a figure wrapped deep in a parka, with the fur-rimmed hood already raised as if it wasn't a merely brisk day, but rather a north polar night. She, for there was no chance of a guy wearing such tight jeans and making them look so good, carried an equally bundled child.

He came up and stuck his nose right into the child's hood, "Tessa, my love! Give us a kiss!"

"Kiss!" the little girl squealed and kissed him on the nose.

Then he rubbed noses with her until she was giggling before he pulled back. He'd ended up standing very close to the woman holding her. He could just see brilliant blue eyes, a freckled nose, and a bright smile in the narrow opening of the hood.

"Do you greet all the girls that way?" Her tone was light, almost musical.

"Sure." Never one to back down from a challenge, he stuck his face right into her hood until their noses rubbed and cried out, "Give us a kiss!"

Unlike the little girl, there was no squeal. Instead, there was a quick squawk of surprise.

Way over the line, Doug.

But before he could retreat, she gave him a quick kiss. Unlike Tessa's it didn't land on his nose, but right on the mouth. There and gone, but the lips were warm, soft, and tasted of peanuts and chocolate.

Once he was clear of the hood, the gloved slap that he expected to follow, didn't. He glanced again into the tunnel of the raised hood.

The bright blue eyes caught the low sunlight and weren't round with shock or narrowed with anger.

"Well," she blinked in slow motion, "okay then."

He laughed, he couldn't help himself.

Now that was his kind of woman.

CHAPTER 3

*C*helsea **had no idea** what had come over her. She didn't randomly kiss men, even tall handsome ones who adored small children.

Men who then scooped a little girl out of her arms, slung her around with the ease of long practice until she was riding piggy-back, and—while Tessa shouted, "Horsie!" with glee—galloped about the yard with a protective hand wrapped awkwardly behind him. The man shook back his collar-length, sun-streaked hair the color of worn leather so that it brushed in Tessa's face. He let out a fierce whinny escalating her giggles of delight.

He trotted up to Mark and Emily then stopped with a sidle and a stomp that was thoroughly horselike and delivered the child to Emily. Then he and Mark made quick work of pushing the plane back into the hangar.

Chelsea was still standing shocked into place when they'd finished and the men had returned carrying the luggage.

"A field pack, very practical," the man who'd kissed her

held it aloft as if it contained only air rather than most of Chelsea's worldly belongings. Her camping gear was stashed at Aunt Betsy's and a dozen boxes of books at Mom and Dad's, but the rest of it was in that pack.

"It's my hiking pack, but I use it for everything. Really practical since I hike a lot," she was rambling; time to cut that out. She sniffed at the air and the cold made her nose hurt on the insides, "At least when it isn't sub-Arctic."

The man's jacket was fleeced-line denim, but he hadn't even bothered to button it against the frosty day. He smelled of hay and his kiss had been warm and fresh with the outdoors.

Mac greeted his son with a firm handshake, but gave Emily a deep hug that surprised Chelsea almost as much as being kissed by a total stranger. What had happened to the woman's backbone of steel? Emily leaned into Mac's hug as if she was the one related by blood and was happily come home. Then he led them toward the house, leaving Chelsea and her luggage bearer to trail behind.

"Do you have a name or should I just shout 'Sherpa!' when I want your attention? Or perhaps *daai?*"

"*Daai?*" he led her onto the wide porch and held the door for her to enter the mud room. There they shed boots and jackets. She was glad she'd been wearing a thick sweater against the damp chill in Oregon and kept it on for added warmth.

The others were talking happily enough together to be lost in their own conversation as they too stripped off the outdoor gear and pulled on slippers from the large basketful of them close by the inner door.

"*Daai* means *older brother* in Nepalese," she explained

softly. "A sign of respect. Better yet, *bhaai* for *younger brother* as who knows if you're worthy of respect."

"You kiss me and question whether I'm worth respecting? That doesn't bode well for the morning after."

Chelsea was preparing a comeback, for she certainly wasn't the one who had done the kissing...or had she been, when she turned and saw the look on his face.

"What?"

He shook himself like a horse again. "If I'd known what was under that hood, I might have spent longer kissing you."

"Skin deep, *bhaai*."

"Yes, but what a nice layer it is."

CHAPTER 4

Doug *knew he was* staring, but how was a man supposed to not? Thick waves of red hair cascaded down to her shoulders. Her cream-and-freckle skin only highlighted the brilliant blue eyes that were presently rolling at him. Her sweater must have been custom-made because it traced and enhanced the slender woman within. The rich green was finished with red zig-zags at wrists and waist. A small but elegant snowflake had been knit right over her heart.

"Frozen heart?" He teased to hide his suddenly dry throat.

She looked down where his attention had strayed. "I called this one White Christmas, *bhaai.* And watch where you're looking."

"I am watching where I'm looking, and very glad to be doing so," his made his voice pure tease. Then he wondered, "You name your sweaters?" Could he sound much stupider?

"Sure. At least the Christmas ones."

"You knit it yourself?" Apparently yes, he could sound dumber. But there was something about this girl—woman. She *liked* hiking? Major understatement. Her pack looked like it had been carried by an entire Army brigade, worn shiny in a hundred places. A very well-used piece of top quality gear. She knew terms of respect in Nepalese and could knit sweaters that made her look like a Christmas delight.

"I—" they stepped out of the mud room and into the living room. Her gasp of amazement echoed that of all who came here. Every ranch guest who entered the main house couldn't help but stumble to a halt.

"Quite something, isn't it?"

"It's gorgeous! A little daunting, but..." she did a slow twirl to take it all in. "But this is right out of a magazine. It's unbelievable!"

The large river-stone fireplace was a showpiece, big double-length logs crackled away on the grate. The flagstone hearth was surrounded by plush chairs and inviting sofas. An upright piano stood by a corner window overlooking the horse pastures and snow-capped peaks. And the high-beamed cathedral ceiling made the twelve-foot spruce that he and Mac had felled up on the northwest slope fit right in. The Hendersons always really did up Christmas. Coils of holly were draped from mantel and piano. Wreaths, garlands, winter-themed quilts on the walls...

"Quite the spectacle, isn't it?" And this nameless woman in a sweater named White Christmas fit right in.

"It's fabulous! My family does a totally lame Christmas, as in almost not at all. Once I got to college, I discovered it and turned into the Christmas loon of any group. You should have seen this poor pistachio tree I decorated one year in Puri."

"Puri?"

"India. On the east coast. I spent a couple months traveling there by train after I left the Himalayas."

Himalayas? Right, well, that explained where she'd picked up the Nepalese. What hadn't she done?

"I try to do up my place, too," he answered. "Same style of construction, but cozier. Bet you'd like it too."

"You do, huh?" Something was amusing her but he couldn't quite think what.

"Sure. I live on the far side of the meadow. I'm the ranch foreman."

"Your…place."

"They gave me a sweet little setup. Two bedrooms. Looks a lot like this, just on a smaller scale. A ranch house in miniature."

"You bet I'd like it?" Her tone had gone impossibly dry.

And her meaning finally sunk through his thick skull. "I didn't mean—" He'd just invited a woman whose name he still didn't know back to his place for a quick— Someone should just take him out to pasture and shoot him.

A wicked smile crossed her features. "Sure know how to make a girl feel welcome, *bhaai.*"

Little brother. Suddenly that really wasn't the role he wanted to be cast in. Not even a little. Because he could certainly picture her clearly in that cozy little log house of his.

Chelsea was curled up in one of the big chairs by the fire with Tessa on her lap. The girl was fading, but not out yet and Chelsea felt completely content working through the thousandth iteration of *Carl's Snowy Afternoon* picture book.

Mark's parents were relaxing comfortably in side-by-side armchairs. It was easy to see where Mark had gotten his good looks. His father had passed on his physique and kindly eyes. His mother Ama was Cheyenne and had passed on dark skin and hair to her son. The three of them together were stunning.

Mark sat on an oak-trimmed leather couch and Emily was curled up against him with a woven throw of geometric tans and dark reds across her legs. She looked as sleepy as their daughter while the others talked about the ranch, and fires that MHA had flown to this season. Tessa had her father's gray eyes and her mother's fine features and blond beauty. When Tessa was grown, the three of them would make an equally stunning trio.

It was so unusual to see Emily relaxed, that it made Chelsea content to remain as long as she could in the room. Emily, the successful senior helicopter pilot of Mount Hood Aviation, the woman always in absolute control of any situation, lying against her husband like... well, like a woman in love. It was surprising and wonderful. Yet another thing that Chelsea put into her Someday List. Lie before a warm fire with her arms wrapped around a man she loved.

No. Scratch that. With *the* man she loved. She still had plenty of time to find him; she hoped. Mr. Wonderfuls weren't exactly hanging about for the picking, but it was a nice image.

It wasn't hard to picture what the man would look like in her fire-warmed daydream. He'd have casually long rough-cut hair, worn-leather brown just like—

There was a soft jolt in her lap. She looked down to see that Tessa had landed face first and fast asleep with her nose on Carl's finished snowman.

Chelsea slipped from the room with her and decided that it was time to put both Tessa and herself to bed before she became any more ridiculous.

Still, it was a nice image as she curled up in a guest room with Tessa on a low trundle bed beside her.

Doug Daniels was a *very* nice image.

CHAPTER 6

"*Can't sleep all day*, c'mon."

Doug went for brash to cover his initial reaction to seeing a sleep-tousled Chelsea hunched at the breakfast table. He'd come in to refill his coffee and check up on her as Emily had asked. It looked as if he'd surprised the sleeping lion in her den.

Wrong image. Chelsea didn't strike him as dangerous, just enthusiastic. Like an Irish Setter. The dark red hair color wasn't a bad match. Except at the moment she looked like she'd been run over by warm bed and a soft pillow, and would still be a while recovering. Or like he'd want to sweep her right back into—

Cut it out, Daniels. But he'd lost a lot of sleep over her last night and her current state wasn't helping matters.

Chelsea was clutching a mug of hot chocolate like a lifeline. She wore a gold-colored turtleneck that proved the sweater hadn't lied last night. It revealed strength aplenty to carry a hiking pack and curves to…

He sighed at his libido's nudge-nudge, wink-wink.

"Where's Tessa?" she looked up at him through a screen of unkempt hair that she didn't bother to brush aside. The ten-foot distance from the coffee pot to where he could brush it aside himself was a good thing.

"They all went into town; took her with."

"I should wait for them."

"They won't be back until dinnertime."

She squinted up at him again. "Where the heck is town from here?"

"Choteau is only thirty miles out, but there's not much there unless you fancy a good steak. They're headed into Great Falls which is eighty each way."

"You sure?"

"There's a note from Emily by your elbow."

She twisted her head to read it without relaxing the death grip on her mug. The long line of her neck was… something he shouldn't be thinking about. Mark and Emily might not be his bosses, but this was their guest. And thinking hot thoughts about Tessa's nanny was wrong in so many ways, not the least of it being that they'd be gone soon. Christmas was just the day after tomorrow; they'd be gone the next day.

"You eaten yet?"

She nodded.

It took him a moment to spot the pan and dish, already washed and perched in the drying rack. Neat and respectful too.

"Good. Dress warmly. I'll meet you at the hangar in five minutes. I need to go up."

"Or I could just kill you and go back to my cozy bed."

"You'd do that to *younger brother?*" he asked in horror.

"Absolutely," but he could hear the grin in her voice even if he couldn't see it clearly through her shield of hair.

"You'll miss a beautiful helicopter ride."

"*You* know how to fly one?" She was quick enough to take in that he must be the pilot and turn it around into a tease.

He didn't even condescend to answer as he headed for the back door. "Four and a half minutes."

C*helsea made it in* four and had spent three of that whipping up some instant hot chocolate in a pair of steel travel mugs.

"For me? Thanks."

When he reached for one, she pulled it away. "Mine. Two-fisted drinker."

It earned her that good laugh of his and she handed one over.

Doug had a pretty little Bell JetRanger pulled out of the hangar and was going over it carefully. Chelsea was taken aback for a moment. Two months ago she knew helicopters were the ones with their propellers on top instead of pointing to the front; now she recognized a JetRanger on sight. Furthermore, she thought of it as small compared to the massive Firehawk helicopter that Emily flew for MHA. When had that happened to her?

The pilot-plus-four-passenger craft was clean, but well worn. It looked well-maintained but hard used.

"I've never flown in a helicopter."

Doug looked at her aghast. "You work for two of the best helicopter pilots the Army has ever produced and you haven't been up in one?"

"I—" Chelsea hadn't known that about them. But rather than look foolish for the lack of knowledge, she just shrugged. "My job is to take care of Tessa. Mark is the Incident Commander Air"—she hadn't even known he could *fly* a helicopter—"so I fly with him and Tessa in the ICA plane."

"A helicopter virgin. Well, you're in for a thrill, honey."

"Watch it, *bhaai!*"

Again the merry laugh as he escorted her into the left-hand seat and made sure she was buckled in.

The ride was a real joy. The cabin heater kept the chill air at bay as they roared aloft. Headsets with boom mics made it easy to hear him as he pointed out the features of the ranch.

He let her look her fill, but she didn't know if she'd ever get enough. The green prairie stretched smoothly to the hills. The mountains broke from the grassland as if someone had drawn a line on the ground and said, "start them here." It was an abrupt and visceral shock. Only as they flew closer did the illusion start to break; secluded valleys intruded deep into the hills with small rivers sliding between sheer headlands.

"I love this land," Doug whispered softly after she'd finally managed to voice her awe at the rugged beauty. "It can be a hard land, but I never tire of looking at it."

"I wouldn't either," she said with a sincerity as if she was making a promise.

"Now who's being forward?"

31

She hadn't meant to be. Then she realized that she hadn't been. It was just Doug Daniel's mind twisting in… she sighed…much the way hers had been.

But the ranch was one of those places that simply felt right. Chelsea would start helicopter lessons tomorrow if it meant she could fly here. Doug flew with such an easy confidence.

"You've been flying for a long time," she finally turned her attention to the fine scenery inside the cabin.

"Navy. Did three tours, six years. That was enough for me and then some. A SEAL buddy hooked me up with Mac."

"A SEAL buddy? Like the diver guys?"

"Sure, Mac was one too," Doug shrugged easily. No wonder he flew with such ease and confidence. Except he didn't look confident; he looked worried.

"What's wrong?" She checked the narrow dashboard that rose on a pedestal between their feet. She recognized about half of the instruments that were like the ones in Mark's plane, but nothing looked wrong on them and nothing was flashing red.

"Lucy didn't come back to the barn last night. And she had a late season foal, so I'm a little worried about them."

Chelsea looked out the windshield but couldn't imagine how to spot a horse in such a vast area. Now at least she understood that Doug hadn't been sweeping back and forth over the ranch and the prairie simply to show it to her; he'd been quartering and searching the ground. She'd done search and rescue for lost hikers, but that was tromping through woods and over rough terrain.

"How do you find a horse in thousands of acres?"

"Well," he pointed down at a lush, pocket-sized meadow around a tiny lake. "I was hoping she'd be here. It's a favorite of the horses. Hold the collective a minute."

"The what?"

"The control on the left side of your seat. Just hold it steady, don't worry, you can't crash us."

She tentatively wrapped her hand around the control, until she had a firm grasp. "Okay," she barely dared whisper it.

Doug took his left hand off his matching control and reached back to scrabble around behind the seat.

Daring greatly, she pulled up on it ever so slightly, and could feel the helicopter rise. She eased back down until the altimeter said she was back at the starting level.

"Here," he dropped something heavy in her lap. "Put that on, would you?"

She opened the case and looked down at the contraption, for that was the only word for it. There were straps to hold it to your head. It looked like a pair of goggles from one side, and like a half-unicorn, half-bug-eyed monster monocular protruding from the other.

"What is it?"

"Night vision. Lucy and the foal will be significantly warmer than the background. She'll show up clearly. Mark gets us the best toys."

Chelsea straightened it out and leaned over to put it on Doug's head.

"No," he stopped her. "You wear it."

CHAPTER 8

Doug was amused by her exclamation when she got it turned on. Chelsea took such pleasure from everything about her. The countryside, the helicopter—rather than showing fear she'd proved she had a good and light touch—and now the night vision was tickling her fancy. Last night he'd left early. Partly because it was a time for the family to be together, but also because the vision of Chelsea with Tessa in her lap had been so powerful. She'd made it too easy to imagine a red-headed girl sitting right there, curled up by his fireplace.

For the next two hours, he flew and she scanned. He filled the time with learning about her background. Deeply independent—with parents who had little interest in an intelligent child filled with dreams—she'd forged out on her own. Six years to get her degree because she'd spent two years traveling and hiking; first walking the Continental Divide Trail from New Mexico to Glacier Park, and then all over the Himalayas.

It both amazed and saddened him. She was incredible,

had a much clearer view of the world and herself than most people. But he'd found where he wanted to be and she had adventure deep in her blood. She'd never be satisfied with…stupid fantasies of a demented ranch manager.

"There," her shriek almost blew his eardrums. Close beside the farthest fishing cabin, Lucy and her foal were huddled up against the side of the building. Lucy was lying down. Not a good sign.

He landed as close as he dared and rushed out to the mare. He'd brought a handgun, but not wanting to jar Chelsea's sensibilities, he'd left it stowed on the helo.

"We won't have to shoot her, will we?" Chelsea was right beside him.

Okay, so much for that worry. "Let's hope not."

Lucy was down, but had raised her head to watch his approach. Her whinny of greeting was encouraging.

He talked to her as he checked her out. No complaints as he tested for broken limbs. Same for the abdomen. Then she coughed in his face, a dry, hacking cough. He felt under her jaw and found swollen lymph nodes.

"Oh, crap!"

"What?"

"We vaccinated her against this."

"What?" Chelsea sounded deeply worried.

He sighed, "She has the flu. I can't do much for her here. She needs a warm barn and some rest. I'll have to ride back out, bring some high energy food and probably start her on a round antibiotics against secondary infection. With a little luck, she'll come back if I guide her. It will be a long slow ride."

CHAPTER 9

They flew back, and when Doug saddled up a horse, she'd insisted he saddle two. She'd never ridden a horse, only a very recalcitrant mule when she'd sprained an ankle coming off climbing Imja Tse. She could have hobbled out faster than that Nepalese mule had carried her.

At Doug's guidance, she'd packed a pair of saddlebags with a change of clothes and several days of food. He packed clothes, camping gear in case they were caught out, horse meds, and a twenty pound sack of oats.

He led off at a light trot and she let him. Her horse, a big dapple gray male called Snowflake, looked at her strangely several times as she struggled to imitate Doug's easy saddle position. Every now and then he'd glance back to make sure she was still with him, and she always managed a plucky wave or nod as the saddle's hard leather slowly beat her to death.

They were about an hour out when he happened to look back during one of her barely-still-on-the-horse moments. Doug twisted his mount in a tight circle like it was the easiest thing in the world. He twisted again until they were side by side. He leaned over to grab Snowflake's reins and everything came to a blessed halt.

"Haven't you ridden before?"

She could only shake her head, because if she opened her mouth she might start crying from all the places she'd rubbed raw.

"You're either incredibly brave or ridiculously stupid!"

"Mostly," she managed through gritted teeth. "Except you got the adjectives backwards." Being at a blessed standstill gave her some tiny sliver of ease. "According to my parents, I'm ridiculously brave and incredibly stupid."

Doug regarded her for a long moment, then glanced in both the direction they'd come and the one they were headed, considering the options. If he tried to send her back, she'd…she didn't know what. But she hadn't gone through this much pain for nothing.

"Okay," he shook his head. "I've seen that look on plenty a stubborn horse and don't want an argument. Stand up in your stirrups, if you still can."

She managed it without crying out.

He unrolled an extra blanket he'd had tied to the back of his saddle. He folded it in quarters, tossed it over her saddle, and then pressed her lightly on the shoulder until she eased back down carefully. It wasn't too painful, and far better than it had been.

"I lead probably a hundred trail rides a summer, Chelsea. You know how many beginner riders could have pulled off what you just did?"

She shook her head.

He held up his fingers and thumb, tips together to show a zero.

"I deserve a prize then."

Chelsea only had a moment to see his grin before he leaned in and kissed her. This wasn't some quick peck through the shield of her parka.

Doug leaned into the kiss and, fool that she was, she welcomed it without even a little protest. He provided plenty skill and heat, but that wasn't what she was really noticing. What riveted her attention was how absolutely her body was galvanized by the simple act. Actually, ungalvanized. She melted against him despite the two horses that separated them. Leaning as far as she dared, she hung tightly onto the saddle's pommel with one hand and his jacket with the other and pulled them together. The kiss ran right down to her toes and made them curl in her riding boots.

When he finally eased back, Doug Daniels looked awfully pleased with himself. Of course she was feeling much the same way.

"I'm not sure," Chelsea was amazed she could even speak, "which of us you were just rewarding."

"At least you won't be *bhaai-ing* me anymore," his laugh was even more self-satisfied than his expression. "Now, let's teach you how to ride. First, take your reins like this."

She did her best to follow his instructions and pay attention, but he'd made a warm buzz between her ears despite the cool day only now breaking above freezing.

Doug Daniels was many things: handsome, male, and a heavenly kisser being only three of them. But *younger brother* he definitely wasn't.

CHAPTER 10

*I*t *was four hours* to the last turn up to the fishing cabin, less than an hour later than he'd planned. Chelsea was the most apt riding student he'd ever taught, and while Henderson's Ranch might be a working one, they made the majority of their income from all of the city folk guests who wanted a week or two of "country." Chelsea took to it as if she'd been born in the saddle… though she'd probably be too stiff to walk right for days. It had been cruel to keep going, but he couldn't afford the time to escort her back even if she'd have let him. He'd bet the chances of that were close to zero, yet another thing to appreciate about the beautiful woman. Tenacious as hell.

As it was, they'd be staying in the fishing cabin tonight. The sunset was only a few hours off and Lucy wouldn't be able to move quickly. It would be a far slower ride back tomorrow. On top of that, keeping Chelsea in the saddle through the night's journey back would be a cruelty, even if Lucy was up to it.

The final lap to the cabin at their quick walk should take about half an hour. Then Doug glanced back over his shoulder—more bad news. A squall was inbound. Blocked by the height of Wind Mountain, and the twisting trail up to the cabin, he hadn't seen it coming. He stopped them long enough to haul on ponchos, but he knew it wouldn't be enough. They were about to get drenched.

They'd galloped briefly on the flat trail, but they were now climbing up a harder route. The way wasn't dangerously narrow, but it would be far more challenging. Another eye at the rain front, now a gray curtain sliding down the mountain face, had him changing plans.

"Ease up out of the saddle a little bit," he told Chelsea. "Lean forward. Loosen the rein. Good!"

And he smacked Snowflake hard on the butt.

He nudged his own mount forward and in moments they were galloping together up the valley. The way narrowed and steepened until they could no longer ride side by side. Doug didn't dare lead from where he couldn't see her.

"Ride on!" he shouted as the first crash of lightning struck the mountain top and thunder rumbled down upon them, amplified by the echoes off the high rock cliffs.

Bless Chelsea, she leaned into it and flew up the trail. He watched closely, but she stayed solid, didn't even a grab the pommel. Her legs must be screaming fire, but she rode, if not like an experienced horsewoman, then plenty close.

The icy rain broke over them, but the trail was solid and drained well, so he left them at the run.

In five minutes they were drenched, but the cabin was in sight. He shouted ahead and they eased down through canter to trot and arrived at the cabin at a walk.

"Down you go," he slid off and helped her down from her horse. "Take their reins and walk them back and forth. It will do all three of you good. Slow is fine, just keep moving." He stripped the saddle bags and tossed them into the cabin. He heaved the saddles inside moments later, then waved her, holding their mounts' reins, down the valley.

Even aching and saddle sore the woman had a walk that stirred his blood. *Ridiculous!* That's what he was being.

He grabbed his medicine bag and the oats and circled around to Lucy who was thankfully back on her feet, but hanging her head miserably in the rain. Her foal was cowering against her. She'd been ten feet from the over-hang and the big box stall, but had been too dazed—yet another symptom—to walk under cover.

He guided them in and checked her. He couldn't do anything for the flu, which was viral, but he gave her antibiotics against secondary infection and a booster shot of vitamins. She perked up a bit for her oats and water. He got blankets over her and the foal about the time Chelsea staggered back up to the stall with their mounts plodding along behind her.

"Is this enough?"

He ran a hand over them. No longer breathing hard, not hot. "You did good Chelsea. Go inside. I'll be in as soon as I get these two settled with the mare."

When he entered the cabin a few minutes later, Chelsea was on the floor in a fetal position.

Shit! He was an idiot.

CHAPTER 11

C helsea had been this cold before, she was sure of it. Like when she'd camped above snowline at the base of Chulu West and the zipper on her sleeping bag had broken. But in her memory it didn't feel colder. And when her knees had knocked together high in the Himalayas, she'd laughed at the novelty. Now she fought not to cry as the insides of her legs, rubbed raw by the saddle, sent shivers of pain right along with the cold shakes.

She opened her eyes when Doug entered the cabin and immediately began cursing. He looked furious! His dark hair matted flat and black with the rain, water cascading off his poncho. He hauled it off with a yank and dropped it on the rough wood with a wet splat.

Chelsea wondered if he was about to tear her to shreds because she'd collapsed, then realized she wasn't the one he was swearing at. He dropped to his knees beside her and began calling her name loudly.

"I'm c-c-c-cold, not d-d-deaf," she managed through rattling teeth.

"I'll start a fire," he jumped up toward the iron wood-stove in the corner.

She tried avoiding the hard "c" of close, but found the "sh" sound little easier. "Sh-sh-shut the door first, you big lummox. R-raised in a b-b-barn."

Doug closed the door and then redeemed himself with his efficiency in building the fire.

"Heat? How long?" she managed.

He looked uncertainly from her to the stove. Not soon enough.

She tried to remove her poncho, but her hands weren't under her control anymore. This was bad.

"C-c-clothes. Off. B-b-bed," she instructed.

He stripped off the outer layers and hesitated until she stuttered out a series of curses at him. She cried out when he peeled her jeans.

Then he began cursing all over again.

She looked down. Her legs' normally pale skin had gone white with the cold, except for the insides from boot top to panties were livid red with abrasions. No wonder they hurt.

The goofball stopped at her soaking wet turtleneck as if embarrassed.

"C-c-come on. You know you want to s-s-see me naked."

He grunted and had the decency to try and look away as he finished the job and then scooped her up like a feather hard against his soaking wet jacket.

"Eww!" Yet even the tiny bit of heat that escaped through the denim felt so good.

The cabin was simple. Three bunk beds, several couches and plush chairs that had seen better days probably back at the main house, and a small corner kitchen with an impressive collection of cast iron pans appropriate for frying fish. Doug dropped her in one of the lower bunks and began piling blankets over her. She couldn't even clutch the blankets to pull them tighter.

"S-s-strip!" Chelsea ordered.

"But…"

"C-c-come on. You know I want to s-s-see you naked," she did her best to stammer it out the same way she had the first time. "I need heat."

He began peeling down and Chelsea watched as much as the shivers would allow.

"Wow! C-c-cowboys *are* built pretty."

He smiled at her for the first time since finding her on the floor. "This is a horse ranch. Not a cattle ranch."

"So get your fine butt in here, horseboy. Before I f-f-freeze to death."

He hesitated at shedding his underwear, someone please explain men to her, then turned away as he finally stripped off that last piece. His butt really was fine; topped by a narrow waist and broad shoulders with muscle that rippled across them with each movement.

Doug slid in beside her and, after a moment's hesitation, pulled her against him. His skin was so warm compared to hers that it burned, but she leaned into it as hard as she could.

"Christ! You're freezing!" He began chaffing those big hands of his up and down her back.

"D-d-duh!" Chelsea managed to get the covers completely over her head and concentrated on soaking up Doug Daniels' warmth.

CHAPTER 12

Doug **held her until** the shivers stopped. With his arms still around her, he could feel her breathing slow. Once she was deeply asleep in exhaustion, he slipped out of bed and dug out fresh clothes from the saddlebags, hanging the others to dry. He stoked the fire, made hot chocolate and wished for coffee, but the latter would make him even more awake than he already was.

A quick radio call back to Logan told him that the Hendersons weren't back from Great Falls yet. Logan wasn't a pilot so he couldn't bring the helo to fetch Chelsea. With the shakes gone, she probably just needed sleep…and time to heal. Gods but she was tough.

The windows were dark with the fading light of sunset happening somewhere beyond the heavy overcast. Lightning still shimmered through the heavy rain, though far enough off that the thunder was a rumble rather than a crack. The weather was still too nasty for a flight even if Mark was back. He had Logan leave a message on the kitchen table so that they wouldn't worry when they returned and found no Chelsea.

"Doug," Chelsea's voice was a whisper barely louder than the crackling flame from the glass-fronted wood-stove. "Come back to bed." The firelight caught the blue of her eyes and the tip of her nose from where they peeked out of the blankets.

"You trying to kill me, girl?" Yes, he'd wanted to see Chelsea naked, from the first moment he'd spotted her climbing down out of that plane in those deliciously tight jeans. Even shuddering with the leading edge of hypothermia, she was beyond spectacular.

"Not girl. It's woman. And I think you trying to kill me once already today should be enough for both of us."

"I didn't—" But he had. He'd taken her skills for granted when she climbed up on the horse. And led her on a grueling ride through a storm. Sending her out on a cool-down walk in the freezing rain was about as dumb as it got.

Unlike so many of the guests who came to the ranch, Chelsea radiated skill. She'd triggered none of his high-season alarms that told him who to watch out for. Though she was certainly triggering other reactions.

"I don't think that's a good idea."

She rolled her eyes at him. "Get your warm butt back in here before I have to climb out and kick it. I ache right down to my joints."

Which told him just how dangerously cold she'd gotten.

Once again he stripped down, far more conscious of

the woman who now wouldn't turn away than the earlier one whose eyes had been partly rolled back into her head.

She went to throw a leg over his, but jerked back and hissed at the pain.

"God I'm so sorry. Let me get some horse liniment," he climbed out of the bunk.

"Hello! Not a horse."

He grabbed a bottle from the kitchen shelf and returned to stand over the bed. How was he supposed to…

"Here," he held out the bottle. "Trust me. It works great."

CHAPTER 13

*C*helsea felt as if she was being a total wanton. She was in a cozy little cabin with no distractions of electricity. A very handsome man, momentarily unaware of his own nakedness, stood close beside her lit by the soft firelight that filtered through the woodstove's glass-paned door. And he was holding out the horse liniment the way you hold out a mouse for a dangerous viper to snack on.

The normal version of herself would have taken the liniment and tried to slather it on under the covers.

Instead, she watched Doug's face as she slipped a leg out from under the covers and twisted to turn it, inside-thigh up. His eyes didn't narrow suspiciously, instead they widened in alarm. She'd watched him handling the horses with a gentle but firm hand. A half ton of horse flesh didn't bother him at all, but the inside of a woman's leg had him totally flustered. Damn but he was cute.

"Come along, horseboy," she coaxed him in the same tone he'd cajoled the colt to follow its mother into the stall.

His gaze snapped from her leg to her face, and then his nice deep laugh rolled out. "Okay, you got me. I'm dying to slather some liniment on those fine legs of yours." And he knelt on the wood floor beside her and smoothed some on.

It was cold and sent a shiver up her leg. But the warm steadiness of his hand stroking in the thick liquid calmed the convulsive response before it could turn back into the shakes. She could feel his hard calluses and easy strength, but was surprised at the gentleness of his rough hands. Within moments a numbing warmth spread up her leg in a wave of relief.

"I'll smell like a horse," she complained to cover a moan of delight. The camphor was sharp in the cabin's warm air, but her attention was nowhere near her nose.

"A sweet smell to a rancher."

"How about to a horseboy?"

"Lady," he didn't even bat an eye. "You smell incredible to this horseboy, with or without the liniment."

There was no sign of any embarrassment by the time he'd ministered to both her legs and tucked them once more under the covers. He'd somehow transferred all of it to her. As he slid back under the layers of blankets, Chelsea was intensely aware of the narrow bunk and the warmth of his body pressed against hers. She was more of a long t-shirt gal, but it would be stupid to ask for one with a man she'd lain naked against for most of the last few hours.

Unable to find words, she simply nestled inside the curve of his arm. Then, against the fiery tension building so high that it roared in her ears, Doug began talking. He told her about the birth of the foal, who slept even now in the nearby stall with Lucy. He talked about the ranch and the spring wildflowers that colored the prairie like a paintbrush.

She fell asleep with the sound of his love for his life rumbling from his chest directly into her ear. It was the sweetest, safest sound she'd ever heard.

CHAPTER 14

He'd *offered to call* the helo a half dozen times this morning, but Chelsea had turned him down cold, despite hobbling about like a geriatric case. Another round of liniment helped some, but he knew she'd be stiff for days.

Doug finally gave in. Partly because he knew Lucy wouldn't be up for more than a casual amble and partly because he wanted every single minute with Chelsea that he could get. He'd held her throughout the night, marveling at the rightness of it.

It had been like that when he'd arrived at the ranch fresh out of the service. After three full tours, most of them spent on ships in the Persian Gulf, he'd been sick to his heart of the unending heat, the limitless steel, and the noise—for a Navy ship was never silent. He'd been on the ranch for three years now and could still feel the Persian dust in his pores. But the ranch had fit him since the first moment he'd stepped on the soil.

He'd ridden plenty as a kid at his parents' place in

Wyoming. When he didn't re-up, SEAL Commander Luke Altman had sent him up to see his own former commander outside Choteau, Montana. Mac had shown him around Henderson's Ranch and Doug had decided on the spot that he never wanted to leave. Mac and Ama had been looking for a foreman. Together, they'd transformed the aging ranch into a showplace tourist destination.

He'd worried a lot about "the son" coming home, until he'd met Mark and Emily. Mark had taken one look at the transformation and thumped him hard on the shoulder before walking away without a word.

It was Emily who'd translated for him. "He was so worried for his parents. You've really touched him." Then she'd kissed him on either cheek. "You done good, Doug. Keep it up." Then she'd gone after her husband. That's when he'd set his sights on the kind of woman he wanted. One just like Emily Beale.

And he couldn't have found one more different than Chelsea Bridges if he'd tried. Oh, a lot of the things that were right with Emily were just as right on Chelsea, especially her absolute fearlessness—the image of her galloping through a thunderstorm on her first ride still fired the imagination.

But where Emily was quiet, thoughtful, and soft spoken, Chelsea spoke her mind and laughed with a bright joy—even when on the verge of succumbing to hypothermia.

He imagined it would take years to fall for the right woman once he met her, because his ideal woman didn't fall that quickly. At least so he'd thought until he'd rubbed noses with Chelsea inside a parka hood and received a kiss for it. Now he was crazy about a sassy redhead who'd slept in his arms like she'd always been there.

Slept. And that was all she'd done. Hard to blame her, as her body had been through a lot of extremes yesterday. But the only extremes he'd been through had been treating Chelsea as if she was his injured sister. Everything had been perfectly chaste last night, if you didn't include his thoughts.

"Storm has passed," he did his best to distract himself. "Temperature is falling and there's another front moving in. Let's get ahead of it."

"Sure," she gamely picked up her saddle, that probably weighed half as much as she did, and headed for the door.

So much for a morning tumble, or even a kiss.

He'd escaped her bed early—because it was either that or he was going to do something wholly inappropriate— and bundled up to go tend the horses. Lucy had perked up overnight enough to greet him. She was still snotty with the flu, but it was clear so no secondary infection yet. Her breathing also sounded clear enough for the walk back to the ranch. The foal was more cheerful than the night before, which he'd take as a good sign regarding his mother's condition. By the time he was back inside, Chelsea was dressed in warm clothes and had made the bed. Oatmeal and coffee were simmering on the woodstove.

She'd looked as natural here as no paying guest ever really did.

They'd had breakfast together; Chelsea going on about the upcoming ride...and he hadn't jumped her. What was up with that? There was decent and there was ridiculous, and he'd definitely crossed that line somewhere in the night.

Then she'd washed the dishes, grabbed her saddle, and gone.

He'd already taken his own saddle out. So, he gathered up their saddle bags, double-checked that the woodstove was secure—the few remaining embers would burn themselves out—and gave the cabin one last look. All ship-shape...damn it. Not a single tousled bed sheet. He hadn't brought any protection with him, but that didn't mean there weren't other options. But had they used them? Nope! Not a single, damned, inappropriately pleasant fondle had passed between them.

Closing the door, he stomped around to the horse stall and ran head on into a kiss.

This wasn't some little kiss through a parka or a taste of wonder when they were both up on horses. Chelsea wrapped herself around him and had him backed against the rail fence. With her arms tight around his neck, she was rapidly killing off fantasy after fantasy. Who knew it was possible to pack so much joy into such a simple act? Apparently Chelsea did.

When Snowflake came over to snort in his hair across the fence, Chelsea flapped a hand at the horse's nose.

"Busy here," she mumbled at the big gray.

Damn straight! was all Doug could think. All that soft and gentle warmth of last night had been replaced by the lively redhead who'd teased with him since the moment of her arrival. She didn't play coy or tease now; she delivered a kiss with her entire body. It left him shuddering with need when she abruptly released him and, as if his world hadn't just been spun around and dropped on its head, strode into the stall with one of the saddlebags that he'd dropped when she'd jumped him.

Unable to trust his voice, he focused on saddling them up. No need to rope Lucy or the foal. Lucy, he knew would follow them, and the foal would follow his mom.

Placing his hands around Chelsea's waist to help her up into the saddle was almost his undoing. With her arms raised to the reins and pommel, her jacket slid up and her waist was slender and warm in the circle of his hands.

Her smile was mischievous as he climbed up on his own mount.

"What?"

"I just wanted you to know, that kiss wasn't a thanks for how wonderfully you took care of me last night."

"Then what was it?"

She turned Snowflake and with a skilled nudge, sent her down the trail at an easy walk. "That," she called back over her shoulder, the only sound in the still morning other than the clopping of the horses' hooves. "That was just a preview. Like coming attractions at the movies."

Any ability to speak that Doug thought he'd regained was washed away. If that was a preview, he couldn't wait for the main feature. But the ranch was a long way off.

He looked back at Lucy and her foal who'd fallen in behind. "How fast can you walk?"

The horse declined to answer, instead settling into a slow shuffle.

CHAPTER 15

"**S**o, *the lost is* found," Mark greeted her cheerfully as Chelsea entered the ranch house kitchen.

"Seems so." It had taken seven hours to walk Lucy back. A long cold ride, but under a broken sky rather than a freezing rain. It was now mid-afternoon and the sky was once again darkening beneath an overcast. At least she'd be cozy and safe for the next storm.

"Tessa's down for her nap, so you can just relax. Where's Doug?"

"He's out at the isolation barn. He wants to keep the three horses and foal away from the herd until he's sure that they're not contagious."

"Good man."

"The best." Chelsea knew she'd never met a better one.

Mark looked at her curiously, and then headed for the door. "I'll just go and check on him."

"Do you know *anything* about horses?" She didn't know where the tease had come from. Women didn't tease men like Mark Henderson. But Doug had told her how Mark loved to fish, and almost always used an ATV rather than a horse to get there, so she couldn't resist.

He just winked at her and was gone.

Chelsea took a quiet minute to heat some leftover beef vegetable soup before sitting with it at the big kitchen table. It could seat a dozen without crowding. The kitchen was on the border between a generous farm kitchen and a small commercial one. It was cozy but also designed to feed a hungry hoard. She could imagine dinner parties here filled with laughter and good food.

"What would it be like to live here?" she asked the quiet kitchen. "How happy would it be?"

"Quite happy."

Chelsea startled and almost lost her soupspoon to the floor. For a startled second she thought the kitchen had answered her.

Then she spotted Emily Beale sitting quietly in a deep chair by the kitchen fireplace, a book in her lap. She rose smoothly and came to sit just around the corner of the table from Chelsea.

"The first time I came here, I was in absolute terror."

"You, in terror. Like I'm going to believe that."

Emily's smile was always a surprise and it was this time as well. "Seriously. I was engaged to my co-commander of an elite U.S. Army helicopter team—seriously bad from a regulation point of view—and about to meet his parents, one of whom had served twenty years as a Navy SEAL. I'd never gone fishing, never seen a horse up close, and never been to Montana."

Chelsea toyed with her soup. "This place is so amazing though; that must have helped."

"It did. Though not as much as realizing that Mark knew as little about horses as I did." Now Emily's smile turned rather wicked. "Mac and Ama bought the ranch after Mark had gone to West Point."

"So?" Chelsea tried to picture Mark not perfect at something and wasn't coming up with a good image.

"Let's just say that he ended up head over heels in the river and I didn't."

Chelsea held up a hand in salute, but was shocked when Emily actually high-fived it. "Women rule," Chelsea added weakly.

"We do," Emily agreed and offered her a smile of companionship that felt as crazy as everything else that had happened in the last two days.

"I've been very happy here," Emily continued though more as if she was speaking to herself. "It's a good place, as good as any I've ever been."

"I'll miss the ranch when we go."

Emily nodded, but was studying Chelsea carefully.

"What?"

Emily shook her head.

"Nope." Chelsea grabbed onto her bravery. "You don't get to do that."

"Do what?" Emily pretended all innocence.

Chelsea aimed her soupspoon at Emily, "Have that clear a thought and then not share it."

Emily considered for a long moment and then nodded at how that might be a reasonable demand. "Just remember."

"What?"

"You asked."

Chelsea swallowed hard. Why didn't she think she was going to like what came next? She nodded for Emily to go ahead anyway.

"It isn't the ranch that you'll be missing."

Her soupspoon slipped from nerveless fingers and landed in her bowl with a splash.

"Thought so," Emily remarked drily.

"Couldn't you at least have made it a question?"

Emily shook her head. "Why would I, when it isn't one."

"But we haven't even—"

"Doesn't matter. When it's the right one, the particulars don't matter. Trust me, I know."

"The right what? But—" Chelsea managed weakly wondering why she was trying to argue. She'd never met a man like Doug Daniels, a man who simply shone with the love inside him. He had such a passion for the land and the horses.

During the long, cold ride back from the fishing cabin, she and Doug had warmed the time with stories. He'd told her about his experiences overseas, so different from her own tramp abroad. In all of her travels, she'd never found anyone so easy to be with.

And the way he'd knelt before her in the cabin, naked and beautiful and so worried about offending as he treated her abraded legs with stinky liniment.

The way he'd held her last night. There couldn't be another man anywhere who wouldn't have taken advantage of the situation. But not Doug with his soldier's honor.

"I—"

But Emily was no longer there to explain things to. In the big kitchen was only the warm crackling of the fire, Chelsea, and a bowl of soup.

CHAPTER 16

D oug was slumped on his couch. The grumbling in his stomach complained about missing dinner up at the main house; too frustrated to whip up something in his own kitchen. He hadn't been able to go because of what else he'd find there. What he was wanting so badly.

The knock on his front door had him racing to answer it. "Is Lucy…o…kay?" The only knock he'd been expecting had been Logan's if Lucy had a relapse. His nervous system was not ready for the vivid redhead standing on his front porch.

"Hi!" Her smile was big and again mischievous.

He had the feeling that he was suddenly in deep trouble.

"Do I get invited in? If not, I'm taking Emily's special homemade pizza back with me. She said that it's one of your favorites."

That's when he focused on the large covered tray Chelsea was carrying. Emily was an amazing cook, had won the hearts of Mac, himself, and every one of the ranch hands with a beef stew on her first visit to the ranch. But it was her from-scratch pizza that blew Doug away.

"Uh—" He looked back up at Chelsea. "I'd like to invite you in, but I don't think that's the best idea. Because if I do—" If he did, he couldn't be accountable for keeping his hands off her a second time. Last night he'd liked the brave and competent woman, and lusted after the redheaded knockout. On the long ride back, he'd also come to admire her deeply. She'd made some hard choices on her path, who hadn't. But hers had always come straight from the heart.

"—If you do invite me in," Chelsea picked up for him as she eased him slowly backward with the leading edge of a tray of pizza, "we just might enjoy ourselves beyond all imagining."

"Something like that," he managed.

"Good. I'm counting on it." She kicked off her boots, and carried the tray through his living room and into the kitchen as if she'd always lived here. "You were raised in a barn. Close the door; it's cold out there."

Helpless to argue, he did as she suggested and followed her into the kitchen.

"I'm sorry," she set the tray on top of the cold stove.

"Sorry for what?"

"The pizza and the tiny ranch house tour are going to have to come later. I can't wait any longer." She shed her gloves and jacket and dropped them to the floor. Then she walked straight into his arms.

CHAPTER 17

They had cold pizza while sitting among their clothes on the kitchen floor. Doug reheated some after they'd made prolonged use of the living room sofa; long enough to have to restock the fire. They finished the last of the meal on their way upstairs when she went hunting for the bedroom; a search that was gloriously rewarded.

"Did we miss anywhere?" Chelsea lay sprawled over him, sore in so many wonderful ways. She'd never done anything like this. Never had so much fun having sex either. Doug's blend of powerful yet gentle, of roughly needy and deeply giving had enthralled and sated her like no one before.

"Uh, big bathroom, second bedroom, home office."

"Oh." They'd probably kill each other if they tried for all of them tonight.

"Back porch lit by June moonlight," he mumbled on. "There's a set of waterfalls with a hot spring about a three-hour hike above the fishing cabin that shouldn't scare off a woman who had hiked in the Himalayas. The open prairie on a warm May afternoon where you'd outshine the sun. I'll show you—"

She put her fingers over his mouth to stop him and he kissed the fingertips.

"I like your imagination," she propped herself up on his chest and looked down into his dark eyes. "So the sex is good."

"Incredible," he agreed.

"You love what you do?"

"I do," he agreed just as equably.

"And you've spent two days and two nights fantasizing about having me beside you forever."

"Yep."

She waited for it. Perhaps it was unfair. Giving a man his favorite food then making love to him multiple times; his defenses were pretty much gone.

But there was no shock of recognition at what she'd just said. No startled disclaimer that he wasn't dumb enough to extrapolate two days into a lifetime.

"Whoa there!" It was supposed to have been a tease.

"As the lady once said," he grinned up at her. "Hello! Not a horse."

"Hold on."

"The way I figure it," she could feel his chest rippling against hers as he spoke, "it's actually been two days and three nights. I think we're closer to sunrise than sunset. So, we've already made it twenty-five percent longer than what you said."

"Douglas," she warned him.

"Just Doug. Nobody calls me Douglas, not even Mom."

"Douglas!"

"Yes, Chelsea?"

"Does it make any sense?"

"Nope. Not a bit," and his voice remained merry.

"Aren't you even a little surprised?"

"Nope."

"Why not?" Chelsea's own thoughts were in such turmoil, they might as well be a wheeling herd of horses.

"Got over it in the barn while taking care of Lucy."

"A *horse* told you that we'd be spending our lives together? Even from horseboy, I'm not buying that one." *Spending our lives together* and still no flinch on his part. She checked in with herself. Even stranger, there wasn't a flinch on her part either.

"No, from Mark."

"Mark?" was all she managed.

"Yep! I was out making sure Lucy and the other horses were all settled in, when he came out to the barn."

"What did he say?" Chelsea was pretty sure she didn't want to know. She went to roll off Doug's chest, but he trapped her in place with a hand resting lightly on her hip. Just enough to tell her she was retreating, not enough that she couldn't get away. *Fine!* She could take it if he could, and rolled back into place.

"He said that you were one of the nicest young women he'd ever met and I'd never find any better. That part I agreed with readily enough," Doug nodded emphatically as if marking such an outrageous statement as simple truth. "And if I was too stupid to see that you were already in love with me, he'd be glad to pound some sense into me."

She let his "love" statement go by for the moment.

67

"Do you think they set us up?" She wasn't sure if she'd be angry or not, but wanted to know.

"My question too. Mark said no. Emily's not much sneakier than he is, so I'm guessing the answer there is also no. I suspect that we did this to ourselves."

"We…what?" But it was lame and she knew it. Emily had said the same thing, or why else was Chelsea here in bed with Doug?

This time when she pushed away, he let her go.

Chelsea wrapped a blanket around her shoulders and moved to look out the window. The yard rolled away into the darkness. Faint lights marked the barns, a lone porch light up at the main ranch house.

Could she be happy here? Working horses, sharing this gorgeous land with visitors? In a heartbeat.

With this man?

Doug slipped up behind her and wrapped his arms across her shoulders.

How was she supposed to know something like that so quickly?

Even if she already did?

Emily had said she recognized that he was the right one for her. As if she knew what love looked like. Well, if any woman did, it would be Emily Beale.

Chelsea leaned back against Doug—and the rightness was there. It ran so deep that she couldn't imagine being anywhere else.

"So I was thinking," he whispered in her ear.

She hummed with pleasure, couldn't help herself.

"How about we just try each other on for size? You and me."

"And the horses."

She could more feel his laugh than hear it.

"And the horses. We'll agree to make no decisions at all until the snow melts."

"But there isn't any snow," she waved a hand toward the window.

He didn't speak, instead he pointed. In the faint lights, she could see the first flakes spinning down out of the sky.

"A white Christmas," she managed on a tight breath.

He wrapped his arms around her a little more tightly.

Doug was right, they needed time to decide if what was between them was real or not.

But she knew. Her wandering days were done.

A white Christmas together.

Chelsea turned in Doug's arms and kissed him. She knew right down to her heart that this was only the first of so many to come.

REACHING OUT AT
HENDERSON'S RANCH

*A puppy at a snowed-in Montana ranch reminds a wounded
Navy SEAL war dog handler that he has a purpose in life.*

A Navy SEAL without an arm is as useful as...

Stan Corman hates waking up each morning to discover
he's lost an arm, his war dog, his teammates, and his calling.
The only thing worse? Going to sleep to face the nightmare of
that single, life-changing moment.

Mark Henderson sends Stan to his family horse ranch
beneath Montana's Big Sky. Not one shard of hope remains
until Bertram, a Malinois puppy left on his doorstep, has
different ideas about Reaching Out at Henderson's Ranch.

Henderson's Ranch now had a structure I could see in my mind. And that intrigued me.

I've always had this weak *restorer* spot in my psyche. I think it comes from when my father's job moved our family (for the fourth time in twelve years) and he was looking for a new house in a new town. During the search, he came home with photographs and floor plans of an old Grand Victorian home that had fallen into disrepair.

For days we studied and discussed this house as a family. We'd have to do most of the work ourselves. If we moved in, for several years every day after school and most weekends would be spent fixing up this grand old place. It filled my head at night and for a long time after we moved into a *different* house—that only needed the removal of some hideous pink rose wallpaper and building out an attic space as my bedroom. I dreamt of that big Victorian for quite a while, hoping someone came along who would care for it.

Now, every time I pass a Victorian or a even a classic barn in disrepair, a part of me wants to take it on and make it happy again.

Chelsea and Doug's adventures out at the run-down old fishing cabin at the far corner of the ranch tickled that restorer gene. I wanted someone to come fix it up.

That combined with the idea that I'd mostly written about a *clean* war in my books. My heroes fly helicopters, fight their battles from the air, and return to bases at night. Some are injured. Some die. But I had never written a story about what came next.

CHAPTER 1

He reached to console the frightened villager child.

Stan Corman knew it was dangerous, but he couldn't stop his hand. His left hand kept moving closer though some part of him screamed for it to withdraw, to fall by his side.

The boy, no more than five, could have been his nephew Jack. They had the same tousled dark hair, though Jack's skin was far lighter.

His hand continued to reach.

Deep inside himself, Stan cursed and fought, but his arm moved without his willing it.

No control.

Except his eyes. Though his hand remained out of his control, he could see with his eyes.

Stan could see the little boy's fear—his eyes so wide that the dark irises were almost lost in the vast field of white. He'd knelt so that they were eye to eye. Then Stan looked down and he could see his dog Lucy abruptly sit, close in front of the boy.

Lucy wasn't supposed to sit without a command unless—

Stan's hand brushed the boy's arm.

Lucy whined.

She was a military war dog and was trained to sit and be still when she smelled—

The boy disappeared in a cloud of light that slammed Stan into the void.

The scream tearing out of his throat ripped him from nightmare to darkness.

Absolute darkness...except for the afterimage of an exploding boy etched so deeply on his retina that it was all he'd been able to see when he woke in the hospital.

Now, months away, he tried to rub at his eyes as his pulse peaked somewhere past skyrocket and began a slow fall that Stan knew from experience would banish any hope of sleep for hours.

But there was no hand to rub his eyes with, only a fleshy stump remained of his left hand. His other hand was tangled in the sheets and for a long awful moment he was sure he had lost that one as well. Before he could scream again, he managed to pull it free and pressed his hand to his face.

Five.

He counted four fingers and a thumb pressed from jaw to forehead. Flesh and blood. He could feel them. Five. His right hand still remained intact.

As did the image of the exploding boy.

Stan's life had been saved because the boy's parents— or whatever total bastard had wired the kid up—had rigged the explosives too low. The alignment of explosive and Stan's life had been almost entirely shielded by Lucy's body.

The helmet had protected his head, the goggles his eyes, and except for nasty scarring on his left cheek, the rest of him had been behind armor and dog. Lucy had taken the hit and like a nuclear blast burn image, the shape of her had been imprinted on his lower face and chest in blood and bone fragments. The rest had healed: the dozen broken ribs where parts of Lucy had slammed into him, the concussion from the wall he'd been thrown into so hard that even his helmet hadn't saved him from that. They'd managed to save his left calf and knee with screws and titanium plates, but had warned him it would always be fragile. Just what every SEAL wanted to be labeled: fragile.

He lay in a cot. His pulse had slowed enough—though the rate of his breathing hadn't yet—for him to feel the hard chill of the cabin. The fire had gone out, which meant it was past three a.m.

It was a good sign. Usually the nightmare woke him by midnight in plenty of time to restoke the small cast iron woodstove for the long, sleepless dark watch. He considered waiting until dawn under the covers, but experience also had taught him to get up and build the fire now or the cabin would stay frosty until midday.

A North Carolina boy, his only experience with true cold before now had been on assignment. The Afghan winters had been brutal, but that's where Special Operations said to go—so he and Lucy went.

Lucy. Shit. They'd been together for two years in-country. She was six months dead and he still missed her every damn day.

He snapped on a flashlight, for all the good it did him. All he could see right now was the little Afghan boy etched in light. The doctors insisted that it was psychosomatic rather than retinal damage because doctors made shit like that up when they didn't know what was going on. The only part of his vision that he could use for the next hour would be in the one dark, dog-shaped patch that had been Lucy in the lower right corner of his vision.

He swung out of his bunk, tipped his head back and to the side so that he could see where he was going, and crossed to the woodstove. Grabbing the handle without a hot pad had him yelping again—not pain but a sharp, panicked sound that rang harshly in the small cabin. If he damaged his right hand he'd be beyond fucked. It was all he had left. He sucked on the slight warmth on his palm as if it was a second-degree burn, cursing the damn stove for still being hot to the touch, but not heating the cabin.

Reaching with his other hand didn't help. The paired titanium hooks of his prosthetic arm didn't care about the heat, but he hadn't pulled the rig on and all he had to wave about was his fucking stump.

Fumbling toward the woodpile, which was on the side he couldn't see, he found a small log and used it to whack the metal handle upward and swing the door open. For its duty and fine service, he chucked the log onto the few remaining embers inside.

Raising one knee, he propped a small bellows on his thigh and pinned its lower handle in place with his stump. With his remaining hand, he worked the upper handle until he coaxed a small snap of flame to life. It was bright enough to shine through the boy's afterimage. Carefully stoking the fire, he watched the flame grow as the boy faded.

The stove wasn't throwing much heat yet; all of the iron had cooled...except the goddamn handle. But he didn't move away. His bare skin rippled with goosebumps, but he remained to watch the flame.

When he'd first come to this small cabin in the Montana foothills, he'd spent many nights contemplating throwing his fake arm into the fire and then himself. At first he only resisted because he knew he'd piss off the ranch owner, and you didn't piss off a man like Mac Henderson or his son Mark.

Mac was a former SEAL—except he'd done his twenty years and retired. Being a SEAL, it was an easy bet that Mac would have followed Stan straight into hell and dragged him back to whup him good for throwing away the gift of life.

Gift of life, my ass.

It was early April. Back in North Carolina, the Sweet William would be blooming right now. The cherry blossoms would have already had their spring and the young cottonwood leaves would be unfolding to seek the sun.

Instead, he was squatting in front of a cold fire in a ramshackle cabin on the edge of the Montana wilderness surrounded by snow. It wasn't the life he'd pictured. But the life he'd pictured had thrown him out on his ass. When he'd gone home, his mother had burst into tears every time she looked at him. His fiancé hadn't even bothered to Dear Stan him. True love hadn't even lasted out the month for the half-man he'd become to make it out of the hospital. His sister had forced Stan's brother-in-law to offer him a pity-job at the bank, as if Stan would be forever helpless. Besides, there was no way he could ever survive working indoors. And young nephew Jack had taken one look at his steel hooks and run away screaming in terror—as terrified as the little boy in the Afghan village.

Then one day he'd gotten a call from his former CO to come over to Fort Bragg. It was the last place in the world for a one-armed former SEAL to be, but saying no to Lieutenant Commander Luke Altman wasn't something a man did.

Altman had met him at the gate, which was a real favor. It saved him having to kill every damn grunt who stared at the hooks sticking out of his shirt sleeve and gave him that you-ain't-a-soldier-no-more look.

"Got someone I want you to meet."

"I don't need another goddamn therapist or perky wounded warrior volunteer to tell me how to live with myself."

Altman had merely looked over at him in that long, quiet way he had and Stan shut up. Altman took him to the SWCS dining hall. It was strange to be back on the JFK Special Warfare Center and School grounds and not be ragged from their typically brutal training scenarios. He hadn't let himself go after getting released, but he hadn't done a decent work-out either—not with one fucking hand. The month on his back had cost him a lot of muscle and the PT hadn't really put it back on—weird to trade the military's Physical Training acronym (or

Puking Torture depending on who was leading the drill) in for medical's Physical Therapy, which told him just how civilian he'd become.

They grabbed trays and went down the line. Stan had learned enough about working his hooks to not need any help. Actually, having been left-handed before the injury, he was almost better with the hooks than with his clumsy right hand. It had become almost natural that when he extended his arm, or flexed his opposite shoulder, the two hooks separated and when he withdrew or relaxed they clamped together tight. Stan used them to load up on he didn't care what and went to sit with another pair of civilians—the ex-military kind by the look of them.

"Stan Corman. This is Mark Henderson and Emily Beale. Former Night Stalkers who founded the 5D."

Okay, that got Stan's attention. The Night Stalkers Special Operations Aviation Regiment specialized in helicopter transport for soldiers like him—like he'd been. He'd flown with SOAR plenty of times, but never with the 5D. They were practically legendary and were always with the very top teams, Delta and DEVGRU. He hadn't known one was a woman, but nothing surprised him about the 5D. If these were the founders… But shit! They were still intact. What was their goddamn excuse?

"They," Altman was still yammering, "have a place that they're going to tell you about. His dad runs the ranch and Mac trained me back in the day. Stan, you're going to shut up and listen."

Shutting up and listening had never been his top skill, but not arguing with his CO—former or otherwise—had been too ingrained, especially when it was SEAL Commander Luke Altman.

And that meeting had led to him squatting naked in front of a woodstove at the far corner of Henderson's Ranch in snowy April.

The dawn had happened at some point while he watched and fed the fire. The purging by flame no longer beckoned to him, but its warmth didn't comfort him either.

He was never going to fit back in. His dog was gone. Two of his team also had been close enough that they'd gone home in a box. The other two had gone down in a hail of crossfire that filled two more boxes. Left for dead; he'd been the "lucky one."

The lucky one.

No team. No unit. No longer a soldier. He'd lost fiancé, family, and town.

There was no one who wanted him. No place he belonged. The dead end was staring him in the face and there was no reverse gear out of it. His future was bricked in as surely as the sides of the glowing iron box filled with ashes and fire. Who would give a shit if the flames did consume him? Easy answer. The future held noth—

A knock sounded on the cabin door. The sudden sound where there shouldn't be any sent him diving for cover behind the woodpile. All it earned him was a couple of splinters before he recovered and remembered where he was.

Furious with himself for sliding back into the black hole of panic and depression, he strode to the door and reached for it with his stump, then yanked it open with his right hand and a snarl.

Ama Henderson stood there with her horse tethered to the porch rail behind her. Mac's wife was a tall, magnificent woman. Her skin was still dark and smooth, but her hair had turned that dark steel-gray that was so unique to her Cheyene heritage.

"May I come in?"

It was a several-hour ride from the main house to the cabin that they'd given him; a damned cold one. The sun…he'd lost time again. It was a couple of hours above the snowy horizon in the crystal blue that was a Montana winter sky.

He held the door wider and the chill wind wrapped around him and reminded him that he was naked.

"Shit! Excuse me." He left Ama to close the door as he dragged on some clothes as well as he could. They were icy cold because he'd dropped them on the floor last night rather than on the chair by the stove. Without his arm on, it proved impossible to pull on underwear and pants.

Hating it, he stood there naked and dragged on a t-shirt first. He couldn't stand people seeing him put on his arm—not even the docs who'd fit it and trained him—but he had no choice. He found the thin cotton sock and pulled it up over his stump, careful to smooth out any wrinkles despite his haste. Then he unsnarled the harness, slipped his stump through one loop and into the socket of the prosthesis. With a practiced lean, he managed to get his good arm through the harness' other loop on his first try, thank god, and shrug it on. Now able to control the spring action of the paired hooks, he was able to drag on underwear, socks, and pants. A heavy jacket against the still cool cabin—he hadn't closed the woodstove's door and damped the fire to get good heat from it—and then he jammed his feet into his boots, though he'd be damned if he'd demonstrate for anyone how clumsy he still was at lacing them.

When he turned back, Ama was sitting at the small table looking down into a bundle she'd been carrying. Kind enough to offer him privacy while he struggled.

"Sorry, Ama. Can I offer you some coffee?"

He kicked the woodstove door shut, almost losing one of his unlaced boots into the fire in the process.

"No. I have come to offer *you* something."

As he'd learned was typical with her, she didn't say much but when she did, there was no point in either interrupting or attempting to hurry her to the point. So, he sat in the other chair and waited.

She looked at him with her intensely dark eyes. "You have decided that you don't want to stay at the main compound. I can respect that. There are times that a man must face his future alone. But there is also a time for that to end. My husband would leave you until spring to stew in your own thoughts. By then the pot will boil over. I do not choose to leave you so long."

He readied his protests that he wasn't fit to be neighbor to man or beast. His screams alone as he rose from each night's dreams were proof enough of that. What if they never ended? What would he do then?

Apparently done with what she had to say, she stood and headed for the door leaving her bundle on the table.

"Ama. I—" he called after her, but the bundle on the

table moved. In the moment of his distraction, she was gone out the door. He knew that even if he rushed after her, she would somehow be gone, departing as quietly across the snow as she'd arrived.

The bundle moved again.

Then a nose stuck out the top.

It sniffed the air once, twice, then the rest of the head emerged and the puppy turned to look at him. Its dark face wore the goofy grin that could only be a Malinois— the same breed as almost every war dog. The same breed as Lucy.

Stan stared at it in horror, not even able to tear his eyes away to look at the door where Ama Henderson had left him.

A dog.

He couldn't even care for himself; how was he supposed to care for a dog?

The puppy yipped at him and he flinched.

It wasn't fair. He would end up killing it just as his one mistake had killed every other good thing around him.

CHAPTER 2

Freshly weaned and only partially housebroken, the dog soon had Stan far more occupied than he'd been on any day in his three months at the cabin.

His usual day's activity was to work on fixing up the cabin—that's how he was paying his rent. It was a fishing cabin in the summer for tourists and it showed. Years of wear and tear had battered the place hard. He'd started with the kitchen. Figuring out how to hold a measuring tape had been a challenge at first but was trivial compared to saws and hammers. With practice, he was getting the hang of it and had made slow but steady progress. Something that had been one motion might now be three, but there was no rush. And once he figured out how to do each task, he moved along well enough. Except the screwdriver was going to send him to the nuthouse; he just didn't have the manual dexterity retrained into his right hand yet.

But the first thing the puppy did once he'd lowered it to the floor—Stan used the blanket the pup had come in so that he didn't have to touch it—was to race around the room about twenty times and then pee on Stan's only clean pair of socks. A second later, the furry whirlwind had chomped down on the leg of a pair of Stan's jeans and begun wrestling them into submission.

He'd forgotten what an insane chewing machine a young Malinois was. He spent the next half hour racing to keep a step ahead of the puppy. He'd pick up one thing and the puppy would discover another. His hand was as big as it was or he'd have swatted the damn thing aside to just give him a single goddamn moment of peace. When his leather tool belt had become the next great find, Stan gave up and let him have at it.

Him. At least Ama had given him that bit of kindness. If it had been a female Malinois, he didn't know if he could have looked at it without breaking down. But like Lucy, it had classic markings. A little smaller than a German Shepherd, instead of a black Shepherd back, it had a black face. And instead of growing into its paws, a Malinois grew into its upright ears and this dog was going to be big—which meant the puppy looked like he was half rabbit.

When the puppy had finally convinced the leather tool belt just who was the king of the cabin, he ambled over and plunked his bottom down beside Stan's boot and began tipping its head one way and another as it inspected the laces.

"Oh no you don't," he stomped his foot, sick of the damn thing.

The pup looked up at him and back down at the boot without startling away.

That gave him pause. "What do you think of this?" He rapped his hooks sharply on the table top.

The pup looked up at the underside of the table for the source of the noise and then its eyes tracked back and forth between him and the table.

Stan rapped again.

This time the puppy watched him instead of the location of the noise.

"Smart little fella, aren't you?"

In response to his compliment it jumped up and yipped in delight. Then it raised a leg to pee on his boot.

In a single motion, Stan scooped it up with his good hand, two steps to the door, and he tossed it into a snow drift.

That turned into another excuse for a dozen circles and then it peed where the front porch post disappeared into the now yellowing snow. It eyed the low steps with some confusion, but had soon struggled back up onto the porch. Once it reached him, it sat and tipped its head as it stared up at Stan to see what he would do next.

Stan looked down at his good hand and flexed his fingers against the strangeness. It was the first living thing he'd touched since the Afghan boy. He tried to wipe off the sensation on his jeans, but the warmth wouldn't go away.

Stan spent some time gazing out at the hoof prints in the snow that proved Ama Henderson had indeed been here and he hadn't imagined her. He looked down. He hadn't imagined the goddamn dog either.

CHAPTER 3

S tan reached out.

The little boy looked so scared.

Five Special Ops soldiers were enough to scare anybody. It was kind of the point. Lucy, fifty pounds of war dog, was no less daunting a sight. Her body armor included goggles against wind and sand, and a Kevlar vest that also sported a camera that could feed visible and infrared imaging directly to a screen that Stan wore inside his wrist. She also had pouches for food, water, and doggie first aid. To the little boy, used to painfully lean feral mutts, she probably looked as alien as the soldiers did. She could work on or off leash, but in the village he kept her on the long lead, more for the villagers' peace of mind than for any real need.

The boy sidled closer as the team eased forward across the village square. It was the edge of evening, the worst visibility for the locals. There was a rumored Al-Qaeda nest two blocks up and one block over. Their team was being sent in to roll it up and look for any intel.

He and Lucy worked to make sure there weren't any IEDs in their path. Check that—they *knew* there were IEDs; it was up to him and Lucy to tell the team where.

The boy came closer, desperately clutching a toy truck. He was close enough for Stan to see that it was a real toy, not just some piece of scrap metal turned into a pretend truck. He knew that was a clue of something, but he couldn't come up with what.

To get down to the boy's height as he edged closer, Stan took a knee—placing one in the dirt, his other raised with his foot planted so that he could push off into a sprint if called.

He reached toward the boy, saying meaningless noises to calm him.

Take them back!

But he kept murmuring.

Shoot him! Chase him away! Scare him! The boy was on the edge of running away in fear as it was.

Instead he beckoned, calling the boy closer, easing his fear rather than adding to it.

No! Run! Hide!

Lucy stepped up close, sniffed the boy, and planted her butt down between them.

He'll kill me!

Lucy whined.

The truck is a bribe! A real toy as a gift to make the kid overcome fear!

And in that instant, something landed on his chest like a hard punch.

Stan swung at it and missed.

Stump. No hand.

He pulled his other hand free of the blanket and grabbed hard onto whatever had hit him.

A sharp yip of surprise and pain. For a brief instant he held a handful of struggling fur.

Fur far softer than Lucy's.

A puppy's fur.

He let go and could hear it scrambling away across the cabin.

Shit!

Stan struggled up from the bedding. The cabin was still warm. He hit the flashlight and checked his watch.

It was one the same wrist as the hand holding the flashlight.

Twenty-two hundred. The dream had given him less than an hour of sleep this time.

But he could see the cabin without tipping his head like the goddamn dog. No explosion apparently meant no afterimage. That was a first.

He went searching for the puppy and finally found her cowering under one of the bunks he hadn't fixed up yet. He had to lie down on the rough wooden floor, which was not all that warm, to reach in and snag the pup.

He nipped Stan's hand, but didn't even break skin. Stan had enough scars from training Lucy and other dogs that puppy teeth didn't phase him.

Sitting back down on the bed, he calmed the pup. Telling it he was sorry. Gods, he was sorry for so much. The puppy forgave him quickly enough, planting both front paws on Stan's chest to reach up and lick the bottom of his chin.

If only Stan could forgive himself.

E arly April had melted into mid-May before there was another knock on the door.

It didn't send him diving for the woodpile this time. It also explained why the pup had gone up on point, but remained dead silent—just as trained. He took to instruction quickly. Usually the first couple years were about little more than socialization and basic behavior. The pup had taken to commands as if born to them.

He bent down to pat it on the head which was now up to his knee rather than at mid-calf where he'd started.

"Good boy." He really had to name the dog, but that would make him too real, too important. Besides, with only the two of them in the cabin, it wasn't as if there was any confusion about who was talking to who.

Stan pulled open the door and Mac Henderson was standing on the other side of the threshold. He was a big man, still powerfully built though he was in his late sixties. His hair, unlike his wife's dark steel, was almost pure white. It gave him a grandfatherly look, but his handshake was still a force to be reckoned with.

"So," he looked down, "that's where Bertram got to."

"Bertram?" Stan asked the dog and the quick thumping of its tail said that the name had found the dog already.

"Ama brought him by."

Mac winked. "Ama's a sneaky one, isn't she?"

"No, she's…" Then he started thinking about the person he'd been six weeks ago compared to the one now. No diving behind the woodpile. Half of the time the pup —Bertram—woke him before the nightmare could take him back under. A couple nights he'd actually just slept through. On the nights it did strike, he rarely woke screaming, though the shakes and adrenaline were still there. He'd snap his fingers and the pup would hop up and join him in the narrow cot and sometimes he could even get back to sleep. Maybe Ama was sneaky.

"Told ya," Mac nodded with satisfaction. "Let's see what you've got done." They spent about half an hour touring about the small cabin. Stan had done more than merely resetting drawers and renailing ladder rungs up to stacked bunk beds. He'd sanded and refinished all of the trim. The kitchen shone. The fine oak that he'd discovered on the bed rails now had a warm glow to them. The gray patina of old wood that had built up over the years had been banished. There was still more to do, plenty more, but he was pleased and so was Mac.

The friendly thump on his back, despite the reminder of the crisscross of his prosthetic's harness, was appreciated.

"I can see that I need to maroon more SEALs in remote cabins around about here."

Stan decided that it had certainly worked for him, when he was sure that nothing else would.

CHAPTER 5

I t was the end of May when the storm hit.

Stan and Bertram had gone for a final hike up into the hills. Two more days and he'd have to move out. The cabin shone, ready for the paying customers to feel they were roughing it out here.

Funny, Stan had just assumed they'd keep him on, give him a place to fit in. In his mind, he'd been sure of it. The itch between his shoulders? Not so much. Could he make it back in nowhere, North Carolina? No. That home was gone. He'd have to find somewhere fresh. Start over. Start over with Bertram? The dog belonged to the Hendersons and was showing real potential.

Shit! Once again he was a half-man with no future. Would he ever find a road to a whole new life? One where he wasn't himself? Apparently not. He had to laugh.

"Too damn scared to try," he told the dog. "Wouldn't that just piss off Altman?" Oddly, Stan realized he would piss himself off too. Maybe, just maybe, he could do this. Find some place…God knew where.

He chucked a stick for Bertram, who raced off through the tall meadow grasses to kill it and drag it back. At first he'd been as clumsy throwing with his right arm as a teenage girl *trying* to look helpless. But he'd slowly gotten the knack of it—the dog had been willing to help him get plenty of practice.

About an hour later, far up beyond the cabin, and the fishing stream that ran close behind it, a long set of falls climbed to an upper lake. They weren't one single drop, but a series of cascading white water separated by brief pools. Bertram loved to plunge into those, despite the glacial-fed chill, and they came up here often.

Today they'd reached the lake for a last look around. A pair of elk, mother and calf, were feeding along the lake shore. He called Bertram to heel. The pup obeyed, though he quivered with excitement as they watched the two goofy looking animals drink and then amble into the freezing lake as if it was a warm bubble bath.

A chill across Stan's shoulders had him turning from watching their play.

The sky to the west had turned dark, almost black. He blinked at it in momentary confusion. To the east, the Montana skies were still a brilliant blue. The cabin was a cheery spot far below. He'd even gotten a fresh coat of paint on it, sky blue with dark green trim, so it really stood out in the meadow of spring grasses and wildflowers.

Back to the west, the darkness was boiling closer and the temperature was plummeting. He hadn't even brought a jacket, just thrown on a t-shirt and gone walking.

Time to get his ass moving. They were at least an hour

from the cabin and the storm would be on them in minutes.

Another glance filled him with disbelief. This wasn't some rainstorm, the ground below the leading edge was turning white. Snow at the end of May? It didn't make any goddamn sense, certainly not in North Carolina or Afghanistan. Sensible or not—it was coming.

He was halfway down the steep path along the falls when it hit. The blizzard slammed into him with hard winds. In moments, it was a whiteout.

Keep moving.

"Only dead men stop moving," one of Altman's favorite phrases.

Bertram was doing far better than he was. Atop his thick fur Stan had fashioned a vest in roughly the pattern of a war dog's armor. It carried water, dog snack, and first aid—a good training tool that was now buffering him from the elements.

The path was soon obliterated and he had to slow his pace. His instinct to chafe his arms proved stupid. Rubbing his left with his right, all he felt was plastic and wire. When he tried the other way, all he got were freezing metal hooks scraping up and down his good arm.

Useless.

Broken half-man.

At the third waterfall, he must have veered off the path. He didn't even have time to cry out before he was plunged into freezing water. The only thing that kept him from going over the biggest drop of them all, were his hooks.

His right hand was already numb from scrabbling

through the snow. But the metal hooks didn't care about temperature and instinct had him jamming them into a crack in the rock. There was no screaming strain on his arm muscles either. The harness took the load and distributed it to the straps across his shoulders. They were narrow and bit in, but they held.

Forty feet of tumbling waterfall crashed loudly on the rocks below. Even if he couldn't see the bottom through the snow, he could hear the water pounding on the jagged rock fall. As he clung there, it struck him just how easy it would be to give up—just...let go. Then it wouldn't matter that he had no place he belonged, he'd be gone.

Then Bertram whined at him.

And for the first time outside his dreams, Stan knew fear. Real fear.

He'd felt anger at everything he'd lost. He'd felt betrayed by his family and by the military. But to die now? To leave Bertram? To not look at the cabin again—a job well done—or heave a branch for the dog to bring back? That would be a tragedy.

He dug in, hauling himself up through the freezing water, mostly with his hooks. He found a purchase for a boot, and felt blessed that he'd finally gotten good at tying laces.

When he eventually rolled up onto the trail, he knew he was screwed. Still half an hour to the cabin even under normal conditions, soaking wet and shivering in the snow. He was going to die of hypothermia right here.

He started to laugh. It was a crazed, hysteric sound, but he couldn't stop it. He'd survived SEAL training. He'd survived being blown to pieces in a remote Afghan village. And he'd survived his own self-destructive thoughts.

A late snow on a Montana ranch was going to be what killed him. Fucking snow.

Bertram licked at his face as if he wasn't already wet enough.

"Why can't your name be Lassie? Then I could say 'Get help' and you'd race the miles back to the ranch in time to save me."

Stan tried going fetal to conserve what little warmth he could, but the plastic arm didn't help.

Then something tugged at his belt.

Bertram. He'd never gotten over gnawing that first belt into submission.

The dog yanked at him again.

"Go away. Now isn't the time to play."

Bertram answered with a hard growl and tugged at the belt hard enough that Stan actually slid a foot down the trail.

"Goddamn it! Cut that out." Stan waved an arm at him.

When the steel connected with dog, he yipped in surprise, then answered with a hard snarl and clamped down on his forearm with a fighting hold.

If it had been his real arm, he'd have torn muscles and streaming blood from the force of the attack.

"Release!" He shouted through the roar of the storm's wind. Great. Snow wasn't enough, he needed a wind chill to make sure he was a goner.

Bertram let go, but didn't back off.

When he didn't move, the dog took a step in again.

"No you don't!" Stan forced himself to move.

"Only dead men stop moving." Goddamn Altman.

But he *was* moving which meant he wasn't dead. For the first time in far too long he really didn't want to be dead.

He flailed out with his hooks, and this time managed to catch the lift-loop he'd stitched into the back of Bertram's vest. It was used when a dog had to be lifted and carried, or winched up into a helicopter. He'd made the loop strong, the one surviving portion of the leather tool belt that a new puppy had defeated on his first day.

"Go," he croaked out the command. "Cabin."

Bertram turned and dug in. He wasn't big enough to make much difference, but he was still a force in the right direction as long as Stan didn't unclamp his hooks from the lift-loop.

At first, he could do little more than crawl as Bertram dug in with all fours. But he finally found one foot and then the other.

He wished he could say he didn't remember the rest of the trip back to the cabin, but he did, every grueling second of it.

His morning cooking fire had kept the cabin warm. And even that remaining bit of warmth was enough to sustain him through restoking the fire, stripping, and crawling into bed.

Unable to snap his fingers, he stuttered out the dog's name and Bertram climbed in beside him. He too was shivering.

Stan held him close, hard against his chest, but the dog didn't complain.

He buried his face in the dog's fur and knew he could never let go. He and Bertram were a team. They would find a way through, together.

Bertram licked at the salt running down Stan's cheeks before they both fell asleep.

CHAPTER 6

"I had this crazy idea."

Stan sat on the verandah of the big house, a beer bottle pinched securely between his hooks, and his good hand rubbing Bertram's ears.

Mac sat on the dog's other side and they both faced out across the ranch. It was now busy with the first of the June tourists trying to prove they could ride a horse around the corral and being shocked as shit that they actually could.

"Let's hear it," Stan was open to any ideas at this point.

"Back in my day, we didn't have the dogs. Left them behind in Vietnam and didn't need them again until Iraq and Afghanistan."

Stan knew about that. The entire program had been lost for thirty years and had to be rebuilt from scratch. Same thing had happened between the World Wars and again until Vietnam. The military swore that wasn't going to happen again, but he knew the main training center down at Lackland Air Force Base was already feeling the budgetary pinch with the supposed end of Iraq and Afghanistan.

"Now the Special Ops dogs, they're special, aren't they?" Mac asked it as half a question. Clearly he already knew the answer.

"Sure. They're trained by select contractors rather than going through the standard Lackland program. We —" Stan practically choked, had to sip his beer to clear his throat. "They, the Spec Ops, need dogs with more skills than the standard program gives them, no matter how good it is."

Mac nodded sagely. He gave Bertram a rough rub on the head and the dog sighed happily.

"Takes a lot to run a ranch. A lot to keep it afloat."

"Hell of a spread you've built here," Stan agreed going along with the subject change. He'd spent the winter and spring out at the fishing cabin. It was only now that he was seeing the horse wranglers, the recreation directors, the kitchen staff, and all the others it took to run the place.

"Still haven't figured out what I'm going to do with that patch of pasture," Mac waved off to the south of garage. "There's also a lot of room to try crazy ideas."

"Such as?" Stan still didn't see where the old man was heading.

"You trained Bertram up a treat," which sounded like another subject change.

"Thanks," Stan wondered when the man would find his point, but he was just as wily as his wife on working his way there, so Stan waited a little longer.

Mac stood up and stretched. Finished his own beer

and tossed it in the small bin on the porch with a sharp rattle of glass.

Stan watched him walk down the front steps and head for the horse barn.

He could barely hear Mac's final words as he walked off toward the barn, "Bertram has five brothers and sisters. Come along if you want to look 'em over." Then he kept walking.

Five brothers and sisters? A whole litter of Malinois? And enough room to train them. He looked at the south pasture again. There was plenty of space for him to build an obstacle course for the dogs. Maybe even a training center for the handlers. Stan could see it clear as day.

He looked at the old man and then down at the dog who had tipped his head to watch Stan and see what he'd do next.

"Bet they barely know how to fetch. What do you think? Want to train up your litter mates?"

Bertram leaning in for another head scratch was all the answer he needed.

He tossed his empty, rolled to his feet, and slapped his good hand against his thigh. Bertram leapt down the steps and they headed out to the barn together to see what the future looked like.

NATHAN'S BIG SKY

This title fits nicely here.

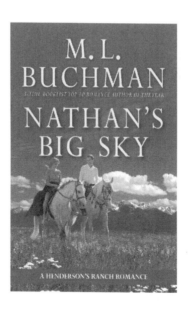

A Montana horse ranch under the Big Sky...run by military veterans Emily Beale and Mark Henderson.

"A really wonderful feel-good story, and a great start to a new Buchman series!" – Booklist

Chef Nathan Gallagher's escape from New York City lands him in the most unlikely of places: Montana. With his past dumped and his future unknown, he seeks something new. If only he knew what.

Julie Larson, former rodeo star and born-and-bred cattle rancher, loves the prairie and the horses. The cattle ranch work with her three brothers? Not so much. The local cowboys labeling her as a Grade-A Prime catch? Even less. When she rescues Nathan from a near-death experience, her future and her heart alter past all imagining.

The only place a New York chef's future and a Montana cowgirl's heart can thrive? Under Nathan's Big Sky.

[Can be read stand-alone or in series. A complete happy-ever-after with no cliffhangers. Originally published as #3 in the series because of short stories that are now collected together in a final volume.]

Grab it now at fine retailers everywhere:
Nathan's Big Sky

WELCOME AT
HENDERSON'S RANCH

When on an assignment to write a travel article about Henderson's Ranch, the story takes the reins from the journalist as a cowboy sweeps her off her feet.

Freelance journalist Colleen McMurphy finds her Irish penname far more professional than the name Kurva Baisotei her Japanese parents perpetrated upon her at birth. Her itinerant writer role fit her deliciously single lifestyle, until an assignment sent her to Montana's Big Sky Country to write an article about Henderson's Ranch.

Raymond Esterling, summertime cowboy, gratefully forgets his life beyond the prairie, at least for those precious months beneath the Big Sky. But when he meets Colleen, he can't help but make her Welcome at Henderson's Ranch.

INTRODUCTION TO THIS STORY

This story was simple, but with an odd connection.

For years, my wife was the indexer for AAA magazine. This means that she received many of their magazines, wrote comprehensive indexes of them, which were then used by the editorial department to make sure they weren't duplicating prior topics. The indexes were also used by the phone support teams to assist AAA members.

What a fun reason to drop a neophyte into my Henderson's Ranch world for an outsider's view.

Here's the weird connection.

Years before, writing my first-ever contemporary romance back in 2006, *Where Dreams Are Born* (the first of the completed Where Dreams series), I had my hero and best friend walk into a Seattle bar. And two women were eyeing them. The best friend particularly liked the looks of one of them but they never got together.

Again, as my brain was searching about in 2017 for a least-likely-person-to-write-a-dude-ranch-puff-piece heroine, it reached back to 2006 and came up with the hip Seattle woman from J&M's in Pioneer Square.

What happened from there, well, that's the story.

CHAPTER 1

Dateline: August 15, Henderson's Ranch,
Bloody Nowhere, Montana

Colleen McMurphy could write this article in her sleep, with her keyboard tied behind her back, and...

"The wife and I had such a splendid time there. You simply must go and write us an article about it." For some reason Larry always went old-school English whenever he got excited—which coming from her Puerto Rican boss who lived in Seattle seemed to be almost normal for Colleen's life.

He, of course, was too busy being Mr. Hotshot Editor to write it himself. That and he couldn't write his way out of a martini glass. He was one of the best editors she'd ever worked for—and as a freelancer that had included a suckload of them—but his twelve-year-old daughter could write new material better than he could. Hillary was named for Sir Edmund of Mt. Everest fame and just might follow her namesake at the rate she was being amazing. She was a precocious little twerp who was so delightful that she made Colleen feel grossly inadequate half the time and totally charmed the other three-quarters.

So, off to Montana it was. Magazine feature article—she was on it.

The most recent in a cascade of ever-shrinking planes banged onto the runway in Great Falls, Montana clicking all Colleen's vertebrae together with a whip-like snap that surprisingly failed to paralyze her. A Japan Airlines 747 had lofted her from the family home in Tokyo to LAX. The smallest 737 ever made hopped her up to Salt Lake, and a wing-flapping 18-seater express fluttered as hopelessly as a just-fledged swallow to Great Falls. If there'd been another plane that was any smaller, they were going to have to put her in a bento box.

But finally she was here in…major sigh…Nowhere, Montana.

She'd used this job as an excuse to cut the two-week trip home in half. Two weeks! *With her family?* What *had* she been thinking? She was going to have a serious talk with her sense of filial duty before it dragged her from Seattle back to Japan again.

Outside the miniature plane's windows the airport stretched away pancake-flat and dusty. Four whole jetways, the place was *smaller* than a bento box. But their plane didn't pull up to any of them—because it was too short to reach. Instead, it stopped near the terminal and the copilot dropped the door open, filling the cabin with the familiar bite of spent engine fumes and slowing propeller roar. She'd spent the whole final flight glaring out at the spinning blades directly outside her window, waiting for one to break off, punch through the window, and slice her in two like one of Larry's martini olives.

"Enough!" she told herself so loudly that it made the fat-boy businessman—who'd made the near-fatal mistake of trying to chat her up across the tiny aisle—jump in alarm. Twenty hours and nine minutes in flight didn't usually make her this grouchy. Her parents did though.

"Why did you change your name?" *Because everyone in America would laugh their faces off calling her Kurva—for the Hokkaido mulberry tree you conceived me under, much too much information by the way. It especially doesn't translate so well for a girl who is Japanese flat. Besides there isn't an American alive who can say* Baisotei *properly.* Kurva Baisotei was not a moneymaking byline.

Then, not "When are you going to get married?" but rather "Why do you not give us grandchildren like your sister?" *My sister has three. How insatiable are you as grandparents?*

"Why do you not return home?" *Because you live here.*

"Ma'am?" Fat-boy was waiting for her to get out of her seat first. Maybe because he needed the full width of the tiny plane, or maybe he was just being nice. She was about to step back on American soil—even if it was Montana—so she gave him the benefit of the doubt and offered a "Thanks" with a smile that hopefully he didn't read as encouraging.

The air outside the airport smelled strange. It definitely wasn't Seattle, which had an evergreen scent that wrapped itself around you like a warm, though often damp, welcome home. Her best girl Ruth Ann always met her when she landed from trips to Japan to drag her to their favorite dive, the J&M in Pioneer Square, and make sure that she got safely drunk within an hour of landing. It was doubly strange to arrive somewhere else without Ruth Ann's patiently sympathetic ear.

Montana was dry and, despite the warm afternoon, somehow crisp. In Seattle there were a gazillion things sharing the air with her: Douglas firs, seagulls, dogs playing in the park, ferry boats—the list went on and on. Here it tasted more rarified. More...special.

Also high on the *special* list was the guy leaning comfortably on a helicopter with "Henderson's Ranch" emblazoned down the side like it had been branded there with a flaming iron. He already had one beaming couple beside him with Los Angeles cowboy written all over their Gucci. He towered above them: six-two of dark tan, right-out-of-a-romance-novel square jaw, and mirrored shades for a touch of mystery. His t-shirt was tight and his jeans weren't bad either. And—crap!—ring on his finger. Fantasy cowboys weren't supposed to have rings on their fingers, but she wasn't going to complain about this piece of the Montana scenery just because of the "Back Off" sign.

Another couple joined them. First-timers by their lost look.

"Hi!" He even had a nice deep voice to go with that big frame. "I'm Mark Henderson. Climb on aboard," and he was helping the two couples into the back seats.

Handsome guy who flies a helicopter. Sweet! Maybe Montana wasn't going to be so bad. Ruth Ann was gonna be wicked jealous. She snapped a photo of him just for that purpose.

"Looks like you're up front with me, beautiful," he aimed a lethal smile directly at her.

She returned the smile, feeling pleased. Then lost it when she realized the implications.

Two happy couples in the back.

Handsome married dude in the front.

And that's when the background research she'd done on their website finally made a horrible kind of sense. Weddings this. Couples that. Family horseback rides the other. Larry should have sent Colleen's perfect sister's family, not her.

She was a single Japanese chick, with an Irish name she'd taken from the old TV show *China Beach*. (She'd always liked the main character—strong woman back when that wasn't a very popular thing to be.)

Be strong now!

She was going to a couples' paradise. This was going to be worse than the parental purgatory.

She'd be pleasant. Polite.

And as soon as she got home, Larry was a dead man.

CHAPTER 2

Dateline: Day Two, Henderson's Ranch,
   Montana Front Range

Montana greets visitors who fly in with the dullest landscape
imaginable. Rulers are tested here for an accurate straight edge
by laying them on the ground.

   But fifty miles to the west, the Rocky Mountains soar aloft,
forcing the eye to constantly scan upward to the bluest sky
imaginable. Henderson's Ranch lies nestled in the softly rolling
country at the base of these majestic peaks.

A night's sleep and Colleen felt much more human this morning, even if she couldn't make sense of what lay outside her cabin window. To the south and east, the land stretched so far away that she felt as if she was perched atop an infinite cliff and at the least misstep might tumble down forever. A person could get vertigo here just sitting still.

To the west, the mountains punched aloft in bold,

jagged strokes with little of the softness that Washington's forests provided to Seattle's peaks.

There was a wildness that confronted her every time she looked at these mountains. Her inner city Tokyo childhood, her rebellious escape to the community of fifty-thousand students at the University of Washington, Seattle's million people—none of it prepared her for this stark emptiness.

Here along the Front Range, aside from a few dozen guests and another dozen ranch hands, there might not be a soul for twenty miles. It felt like a thousand.

Down the slope, a tall woman stepped out of the back door of the main lodge and rang a giant steel triangle just like in an Old West movie: *clangety-clangety-clangety-clang.*

Families and couples streamed out of the other cabins and headed downhill toward the massive two-story log cabin structure that looked like one of those Depression-era lodges. Huge, powerful, unmoving.

A quick survey showed that she was the only singleton —if she didn't count kids, and even they seemed to come in packs. Almost everyone was dressed in K-Mart Western, or some designer version that looked no more likely.

There were breakfast fixings in her cabin, and she was tempted to retreat there, but she was here to write a travelogue article. For that she had to experience the experience.

She was last down the trail to the big house. The guests were all guided along the wrap-around porch to the front entrance into the big dining room she'd seen on last night's welcome tour. Thirty people could eat communal style at the long table.

However, a few others were coming around to the kitchen door. They were dressed far more casually, and far more authentically. Cowboy boots, dusty jeans, a variety of hats—some battered cowboy, some baseball-cap redneck. The women were dressed much the same.

Not really paying attention to what her feet were doing, she fell in with the ranch hands and found herself in a massive and beautiful kitchen. The hands were making use of one of the sinks before gathering at a smaller version of the big communal table out front.

"Mornin', Colleen. Not up for our 'Happy Couples' breakfast?" Mark the pilot greeted her with an understanding smile, reading her too easily.

Time to gear up the pleasant-reporter face.

He wasn't any less handsome this morning, but a stunning blonde kissed him on the cheek as she topped up his coffee, confirming that the ring wasn't just for show.

"Not so much, if that's okay."

"Take a seat. Dad's this one, Mom's the other end, when she bothers to sit down. The rest are up for grabs."

She took a seat almost, but not quite, at the middle of the table on the far side. It gave her the best view of what was going on and would let her hear most of the conversations without being the center of them. No one so much as blinked an eye as she joined them. A pretty redhead gave her a South California, "Hey!" Her husband was more the quiet-nod type.

Another long blonde gave her a very authentic sounding, "Howdy!" just as the male cook (with a Brooklyn-tinged "Hello and welcome") came and set a plate in front of the blonde, then kissed her on top of the head.

Shit! She was in Couplandia here as well. Finally some more guys came in until there was a fair balance of single men. More what she'd expected.

Her goal of keeping track of the conversations went out the window in the first ten seconds. They were talking about the day to come and what they knew about the guests, but doing it in a handful of simultaneous discussions: "Most of this lot we won't get out of the corral for a couple days." "Did you see that absolute babe from England? Never saw a woman sit a horse so *purty*. She'll ride far and hard." His companion—alike enough to be his twin—gave him a knowing smile that was all about the woman and not so much about how she sat.

Colleen stayed focused on her meal and her article. The food was incredibly good despite how basic a hash brown-and-ham scramble with a biscuit buried in gravy sounded. Article ideas were perking up as she enjoyed the camaraderie around the table. These people liked each other. Liked working together. And whatever else they were saying about the guests, none of it was bitter or caustic. She'd expected some derision of "city cowboys" but nothing even remotely like that came up in any of the several threads she was able to follow.

She wondered what they'd be saying about *her* behind her back.

"I like the way you listen."

It took her a moment to rewind the comment because it was only the last word that actually caught her attention. She finally traced it (nearly accentless) to the man across the table. He wasn't a big man—Colleen had an absolute weak spot for big men, who thankfully often had a weak spot for petite Japanese women—but he had a nice smile so she wouldn't hold his normalness of height and build against him.

"Uh-huh," her cordial-meter was still running below normal, but then no one was supposed to see through her pleasant-reporter face. She really needed another mug of tea.

"Heard you just arrived from Japan. Family there?"

"Uh-huh," her cordial-meter bottomed out. That was a reminder that she didn't need.

"Apparently the wrong question."

"Uh-huh," she dialed up her emphatic-sarcasm mode to full.

"Do you ride?"

Her first temptation was to go to "uh-uh" but she already was being subverbal far beyond her norm. Besides, it was the easiest response. Like writing, the easiest word (the first word she thought of) was rarely the most precise or evocative one. Good writing required avoiding the obvious while still telling the story—whether it encapsulated what it was like to work on the Boeing manufacturing line like her last article or the current purgatory of Couplandia.

Her interlocuter (yes! her vocabulary was finally coming back online) looked like a nice enough guy. Cowboy lean with a pleasant smile. She supposed that she'd have to ride a horse to get the full "Henderson's Ranch" experience and a private lesson sounded far better than shaming herself in public.

"Not yet," she added a smile which she knew was one

of her strengths. The guy returned with a powerful one of his own.

It was only then that she noticed Mr. Handsome-with-a-ring Henderson rolling his eyes at her—at least that's what she assumed he was doing behind his ever-present shades.

Okay, maybe she could have been a little more subtle. But he said he liked the way she listened—one of the skills she was most proud of. That bit of insightfulness was going to earn him a lot of leeway.

CHAPTER 3

Dateline, Day Four—

Colleen turned on a light against the fading day and flipped back through her notes again. Where had Day Three gone? Where had Day Two gone for that matter?

She finally found Day Two.

Mac Henderson, technically Mark Henderson, Sr. and almost as handsome as his son, had been thrilled to have her on the ranch. Apparently she was their first journalist, so their resort had a lot riding on making her happy—though he acted as if he was simply glad *she* was here, not several million readers AAA magazine would be sending this out to. Which was sweet of him to pretend.

On Day Two, he'd toured her about: cabins, yurts, cooking classes, weaving classes, horseback riding, even a military dog trainer named Stan—a big, gruff man with a hook prosthetic on one arm who only spoke to his dogs.

As the day had progressed, Mac had grown more and

more excited about showing her around his ranch until he was as wound up as one of Stan's puppies. A former Navy SEAL in his sixties who almost wriggled with delight. She'd always thought SEALs were supposed to be broody and stoic, but Mac was a thoroughly pleasant guy who clearly loved this land with a passion.

What she'd found truly unbelievable was the amount of work it took to run the place, and Mac made sure that she had a chance to meet and chat with every person of the staff. The redhead who ran the barn was so voluble that Colleen couldn't have gotten down one word in ten no matter how fast she took notes—and she was fast. Her husband, the ranch manager, was laconic to the point where Colleen wondered if people catnapped between his sentences.

It took her a while to catch on that he was teasing her with it.

Day Two afternoon: Mark's wife Emily took her on a solo helicopter flight over the ranch that was stunning in both its expansiveness and its variety. The softly rolling landscape around the buildings gave way to rugged prairie, patches of pine forest, and even waterfalls along a small river that ran down out of the hills. A group of horses out at a remote fishing cabin revealed that at least some riders had made it past the corral.

The cook wasn't a cook at all—he was a dropout New York chef...one she'd actually heard of.

She was getting why Larry and his family had gone nuts over the place, but that didn't explain what had happened to her notes. She was sure she taken more of them.

Day Three's notes were definitely not here. Then she remembered…

Raymond Esterling, her Day One breakfast companion.

Who liked the way she listened.

That's what had happened to Day Three.

…and most of Day Four.

Colleen sat down abruptly on the bed in her small cabin. She ran a hand over the bedspread: Cheyenne weaving done by the owner's wife. She was one of those tall, majestic Native American women that never actually existed in real life. The blanket's geometric reds and golds were as warm as the campfire they'd all sat around while burgers were cooked over open flame on a heavy iron grill earlier this evening—some of the best beef she'd ever tasted.

Whatever in the wide, wide world of Montana was happening to her? A good girl's education in being Japanese hadn't prepared her for this place. Nor a journalist's.

Her ears rang in the silence. No cars at night, no planes. Not even the ocean when she vacationed down at Cannon Beach, Oregon and could pretend the waves were actually the low rumble of I-5 that was never silent in Seattle—easily audible from her apartment on the other side of Lake Union.

A soft whinny drew her back to her feet and out onto the cabin's porch.

Raymond sat astride a big roan—as she'd learned to call his cream-colored mount with dark legs and mane. The sunset lit his gentle face.

He'd "happened" to more than her notes. He was happening to her and none of her training, neither as Kurva Baisotei nor Colleen McMurphy, was ready for it. Not even the city pickup bars had prepared her for him— not even the good ones (if there was such a thing).

Worse, Raymond hadn't resisted her journalistic inquisitiveness.

(*Anta, sensakuzuki,* her sister would curse under her breath—*you are always so nosy,* with the *anta* insult thrown in.)

Raymond hadn't resisted it because she hadn't unleashed it on him. Which was totally unlike her. But he had impressive listening skills as well.

To his credit, after his horseback riding lessons yesterday and today—in between the lessons he was giving to others—she had a good feel for riding. This afternoon she'd joined a trail ride for beginners and even cantered once; which had been both exhilarating *and* nearly scared her back into the womb.

But she knew so little about him.

He didn't seem to mind talking—he wasn't a reclusive *hikikomori* or even a male jerk "not in touch with his feelings." But it was as if his life beyond the boundaries of the ranch stretched as empty as the scrub prairie.

She knew that was total crap—he was a summer instructor and trail guide, no more. But every time she got ready to pin him down on what he did the other eight months of the year he'd smile at her, adjust her "seat" position, point out an eagle soaring on a thermal, anything to distract her…without appearing to distract her.

Now he sat astride his horse not five feet from the porch of her cabin, looking the quintessential "cowboy in the sunset."

"You can't be some mystic cowboy forever, you know?"

"Evening to you too, Kurva." Somehow he'd gotten that out of her. He also managed to say it like it wasn't a comment on her figure, or rather lack of one, so she let him use it. Instead, he turned her name into a tease, a friendly nickname that didn't chide her for choosing another.

"Evening to you, Raymond. What are you doing up on a horse at this hour?"

"Hoping to take you on an evening ride and see the stars. It's a warm night, but you might want a jacket." Never quite a question, yet not a statement either. As if coaxing her along like a reluctant horse. She didn't appreciate the metaphor but couldn't find the urge to fight it either.

Her own mount, a patient bay named Gumdrop of all silliness, trailed behind him on a lead. Colleen was really getting the vernacular down. She wanted to do a little horse-words rap there on the porch but resisted it. Instead she grabbed a polar fleece off a hook inside the door and climbed up into the saddle.

Seattle girl in the saddle girl
*Astride some rawhide like a way cool—bri—*No!

Her mind nearly strangled itself when her inner rap

artist cast up "bride" for worst-rhyming-word-choice-of-the-century award. Definitely not!

The vertiginous Big Sky of Montana expanded even more as they rode up past the cabins and over the rise at a lazy, side-by-side plod. Gumdrop's head bobbed easily, no longer nearly jerking Colleen out of the saddle each time the horse leaned down to crop some grass as they went along.

In the sky, golds found reds.

Reds hinted at impending purples.

Soon Raymond reined to a halt and pointed to the west, "Venus."

Colleen didn't know where to look.

Raymond pulled his mount close beside her so that she could easily follow the line of his pointing arm.

It took her a moment to pick the sparkling point of light out of the red-gold sky, then she had it. It hung above the silhouetted-black mountains like a diamond.

"Planet light, planet bright, First planet I see tonight, I wish I may, I wish I might, Have this wish I wish tonight." Ray's voice was as soft as the call of a passing bird. "Meadowlark," he filled in for her.

"This seems to be the sort of place that wishes come true." It really was. The pale dry grass lay in golden waves over the rolling prairie. Far below—she didn't realize they'd wandered so far as she had watched the shifting light—lay the cozy cluster of ranch buildings: lodge, barns, and cabins. The next farm over, a big-spread cattle ranch, was just barely visible and looked homey as well.

"What do you wish for, Colleen Baisotei?" He said it right. It was as if he couldn't quite leave her names alone but had to play with them like cat toys. It seemed to make him happy to do so and, curiously, it didn't bother her. Words were her toys as well. She liked that in a man.

"What do I wish for? Not this."

"You don't?"

"Not really. The beauty here is like a drug. Perhaps in small doses, but I'd miss the city too much as well."

"I know," his voice was as soft as the night. "I come here for the summers, retreat to my city in the fall. But I don't think about that now. Now, I am simply here."

"A cowboy."

"They let me play at being one."

Colleen liked that about him, too. He knew what he himself was, even if she didn't know what he was in the real world. And now she understood why. Whereas she— "Huh!"

"What?"

"I'm...not sure what to wish for." Peace with her parents? There was a greater chance of a forest fire in Antarctica. Finding... Colleen didn't know what to plug in there. That bothered her. She really should know.

Sure, she was doing fine. She had good friends in Seattle, whether for a quiet dinner or to go out dancing: square dancing at the Tractor, Britpop Thursday at the Lo-Fi, or bottom-trawling at the J&M. Her job sent her traipsing up and down the Northwest until she knew it like the back of her hand, but kept discovering new things there anyway. Men were pleasant and easy. She knew there was a type of man who looked at her and melted, and she didn't mind that either. Slim-Japanese-with-dark-hair-well-down-her-back slayed them...another advantage to America over Japan where she was just another potential housewife. Dressing in a tight tube-top at least doubled her yield.

But what to spend an actual wish on…

She turned to him, "What's yours?"

"I would think that was obvious from the moment you walked into the ranch kitchen, Ms. McMurphy."

And when he said it, it was.

She turned from the diamond light of Venus to inspect Raymond Esterling, itinerant horse guide and otherwise unknown. He was what she wasn't. Melting-pot American versus pure-blood Japanese. Sandy blond and fair skinned. Easygoing to her own hyper tendencies—though those seemed to go quiet around him.

"I didn't come here looking to be a summer cowboy fling." Yet he'd grown on her enough over these last days to make it a reasonable consideration.

"Can't say that I've ever been much for flings myself. Every time I try them, I get burned."

"But you're willing to try me? I burn men baaaad! Just warning you."

"I expect, despite my mortal fear of fire, that you are well worth the risk." He also knew how to slay her with a simple piece of flattery. It might be a line, but it was a good one.

"Let's find out."

Dateline...uh...unknown.

Lying naked in the bed, the cool Montana morning washes in the open window and over my body raising goosebumps. The crickets called through the night, singing a chorus of heat that had indeed scorched between the two highly-compatible humans. Now the siren call of the rising sun drags me back to the present.

For five more fun-filled days, and five enchantingly rigorous nights, Henderson's Ranch had delivered. She'd fished, learned to cook her trout on a heated rock by a wilderness campfire (though she'd passed on learning how to gut and clean the fish), gone horseback on a wildlife photo safari (she'd bagged a fox, two elk, and a rare bobcat with her camera), and even discovered some skill with a bow and arrow.

She'd also unearthed a bottomless need for how Raymond Esterling could make her feel.

Feel?

Dear gods, it was like she hadn't known the meaning of the word. Her body had responded to his in ways she'd never imagined. His hand on her calf as he checked her stirrup was enough to wrap her entire body in a warm heat. Even now it burned through her memory despite his having left her bed to start his morning chores.

And what she felt inside was equally foreign.

Demanding that her journalistic objectiveness chronicle what was happening to her resulted in—no answers.

Instead, like the splash of cold water that sent her scrabbling for the covers, she was reminded that her idyll was done. This was Last Day, Departure Day.

By this evening she'd be at SeaTac airport, waiting for her best friend Ruth Ann to pick her up and get her good and drunk. Except she didn't feel the need to. Ray had somehow purged her soul of her parents far more than the most exotic cocktail. Going trawling for a bedmate at the J&M, after she'd had a taste of what Ray could make her feel, would be beyond pointless.

Yes, he could make her feel. And by his desperate groans and happy sighs, she knew she did the same in return.

They'd started their final night together with another sunset ride. This time he'd brought a blanket and they'd made love together under the stars. Once before, she'd done it outdoors, fast and desperate on Golden Gardens beach at a college bonfire party, the fear of imminent discovery adding to the hurry.

Last night had been a slow, languid adventure under a brilliant canopy of starlight. When the half moon rose, it had turned the prairie pale yellow and was more than bright enough for them to appreciate each other visually as well as physically. She'd come to like the way Ray looked, a great deal. He was lean but strong. And only six inches taller meant that instead of her face being crushed to a man's chest when they embraced, she could lay her head on his shoulder and nestle against his neck.

She was a journalist because she loved learning new things.

The things Ray had taught her she could place in no article, but they'd been written indelibly upon her skin and emotions.

But now it was time to go. Showered and packed, she was surprised at the hugs she received after breakfast. The women in particular made a point of saying how glad they were to have met her. It felt genuine.

There! That was the hook on her travelogue about this place.

It didn't feel genuine—it *really was* genuine.

She might have become closer to the staff than the tourists, but as they all gathered together for departure, there were many warm farewells.

Colleen stood in the midday-flight time group, waiting for the helicopter to return from the morning-flight group. New arrivals were inbound for their own adventures, welcomed, and were escorted to their freshly cleaned cabins.

Then Ray arrived and cut her out of the herd. She went willingly until they were alone with the horses in the barn.

"Kurva Colleen. May I see you again?"

"Gods, please, yes. But I'll be in Seattle."

"So you said. I'll come looking for you there when I'm done being a cowboy."

"You'd better."

His kiss made that promise as the distant thrum of the helicopter approached to whisk her away.

CHAPTER 5

Dateline, done.

Larry loved the piece. For the first time, it passed beneath his evil editor's pen without a single tick-mark or correction. Her next assignment started tomorrow, learning about building boat sails. There were several premier sail lofts in Seattle and she had a very nice contract to write a multi-page marketing-promo article about them for one of the glossy magazines.

But she didn't care about any of that.

She cared about the simple text message, "J&M, 8pm. R"

It would be good to just sit with Ruth Ann, drink a Mai Tai or a Mango Daiquiri, and catch up. She'd been back two weeks. Back? As if time was now measured in distance from Montana.

Out of habit and the lingering Seattle summer heat—rather than thinking about attracting men—she wore a clingy tube-top, short shorts, and sandals, and brushed her hair out long. For once it wasn't about torturing men or even finding one.

She'd already found one, and was discovering that she wasn't getting over him as she'd expected. Her some-times-cowboy was persevering in her thoughts—like a good story that was hard to forget. Somehow, she couldn't quite remember how, she'd let him slip away without any way to contact him. He was always good at using distraction. Perhaps he hadn't wanted to keep in touch.

Colleen had considered calling the ranch, but he would be gone soon. The short Montana summer was ending. With the start of school, their number of guests would plummet and the extra hands wouldn't be needed. Yet some part of her waited.

She went with the familiar J&M daiquiri for coolness. She also managed to snag her and Ruth Ann's favorite table. It was small, but close by the door. It offered a good view of the male wildlife down the long bar as well as at the small streetside tables outside the windows. A hundred-and-thirty years of drinking had happened here (with a one-year hiccup in '09 that had been devastating until a new owner was found), and she could feel the history every time. It was deep and solid.

The band in the back was just getting rolling. Coun-try-rock tonight. In another hour, conversation would approach the impossible and everyone would move onto the dance floor. For now, shouting was only necessary in the deeper sections of the bar, and the dancers still had room to do some moves.

The parade of men and women through the door barely registered on her. She could see that she was regis-

135

tering on them, but that was the point. Dates were having to poke their men in the ribs, some of them sharply, to keep them moving.

Then one man arrived by himself—which wasn't unusual.

Dressed in typical Seattle: sneakers, jeans, and a UW Huskies t-shirt.

But his gait was odd.

As if he'd just...gotten off a horse.

Ray smiled down at her as he strode up to the table like he was still roaming the prairie.

"You're not 'R.'" But he was. Not Ruth Ann. Raymond. She hadn't even looked at the sender on the message.

"You told me you liked this place."

"I do," then she caught herself and patted the seat beside her. "Now I really do."

"And I thought you were dressed that way for me." He sat beside her.

"No, just to torment passing strangers."

"I'm hurt. But it definitely works. You're absolutely killing me."

"What are you...?" His t-shirt registered. "Huskies? You're an alum?"

"Not exactly."

She knew there were adult students, but he didn't act like a student.

He cleared his throat as if preparing to lecture.

He worked there!

"UW Professor Raymond Esterling, specializing in advanced robotics, particularly communication protocols with natural language. That means how robots and people speak to each other."

"You like the way I listen," she recalled the very first thing he'd ever said to her. Of course he would appreciate that.

His nod was easy as he ordered a beer from a passing waitress, as if it was as natural as could be. Of course, she liked the way he communicated too. Except when he evaded her.

"You knew all that time that I was from Seattle and you didn't say anything?" A part of her that had been strangely quiescent over the last two weeks stirred to life. Like one of the Front Range's hibernating bears starting to wake up. She didn't know yet if she was of the angry variety.

"That's a separate part of my life. My days in this life are pretty intense. All indoors, a lot of computer code, with some mechanics and theory stirred in. For three months every year I get to ride horses and look at the horizon."

"And snare willing ranch guests."

"Tally of one so far. But based on that narrow statistical sample, I'd say it was absolutely worth the risk. Don't you agree?"

The last, gentle words were so soft they barely cleared the noise level that the J&M was pumping itself up to.

Raymond Esterling. Robots and horses. He took her hand and the warmth ran up her arm and wrapped around her. Not just her limbs, but that strange place inside where no man had ever belonged.

Belonged.

Something she'd never done. Not in Japan, not really in Seattle. Always a barfly never a...she let the next word come after only briefly shying away. Never a bride.

Yet whether enjoying each other's bodies, riding through the sunset together, or just sitting here knowing they'd be on the dance floor soon, she now knew what the belonging meant.

For outsiders, Henderson's Ranch was about welcome —maybe having a place for a week, or a summer. But with Ray, he made it easy to imagine so much more. There was an absolute rightness that was undeniable.

She leaned in to kiss him. Just before their lips met, she whispered.

"Now I know what to wish for. And yes, absolutely worth it."

BIG SKY, LOYAL HEART

This title fits nicely here.

No longer serving as a military dog handler, does nothing to prepare a woman for what comes next.

Recently retired as from working with Delta Force war dogs,

Lauren Foster sets herself a simple mission: forget about the Army, get back to New York City, and try to become a civilian—three missions she's doomed to fail.
Film student turned cowboy Patrick Gallagher just keeps moseying through life—until the woman of his dreams threatens to ride off into the sunset without him.
Named for Rip van Winkle, trainee military war dog Rip naps in the Montana sun—while awaiting inspiration.
Now, Lauren must escape before she gets caught by the love of a dog and a man under the Big Sky.
[Can be read stand-alone or in series. A complete happy-ever-after with no cliffhangers. Originally published as #5 in the series because of short stories that are now collected together in a final volume.]

Grab it now at fine retailers everywhere:
Big Sky, Loyal Heart

FINDING HENDERSON'S RANCH

Holding onto dreams brings them to life!

Mac Henderson started out being no more a ranch owner than he did being a Navy SEAL. Adrift on the post-college tide of the '70s, with no direction planned, he headed west to surf. But fate had other plans for him.

A broken starter motor during Cheyenne Frontier Days led him to witness Ama's traditional dance for her tribe. Since that moment, for twenty years, she has believed in his dream, inspired him, and given him a son (Mark Henderson).

It was only when Mac retired that she found her own dream. Her reward? Finding Henderson's Ranch beneath Montana's Big Sky.

INTRODUCTION TO THIS STORY

I can blame this story completely on a fan! Thanks, Elf!

She wrote me a note one day asking, "Shouldn't that be Hendersons' Ranch, not singular Henderson's?"

Well, it should have been. It was Mac and Ama's ranch. It was Mark's home as well and, after the events in *Big Sky, Loyal Heart,* it was Emily's too.

But I didn't like the idea of it being a mistake that I'd have to fix everywhere and cause, at least myself, a lot of confusion—by this time I'd probably typed it singular a thousand or more times. I even typed it wrong in the sentence above and had to go back and make it plural.

This meant traveling back to the origins of Henderson's Ranch. But that wasn't far enough. How did two people as different as Mac and Ama get together to create Mark and have this life?

There were very few clues in all of the prior books. Ama was almost invisible outside of that one paragraph back in *The Night Is Mine.* Her silence is her defining characteristic, but I never understood why until I wrote this story.

And it was that silence that allowed her character to truly shine in the final novel.

CHAPTER 1

Mac Henderson didn't know whether to hate himself or the Top 40 station coming out of Cheyenne. In Wyoming it was that or country, so the choice of what to listen to wasn't hard. But the songs were insidious. How was it possible that he knew every word to sing along with John Travolta's *You're the One That I Want?* Mac did have to fake the high notes which perhaps implied he wasn't a complete "Lost Cause" his mother always accused him of. She said it with a smile, but still, it stung.

More importantly, how did Travolta get up there? Maybe it was those tight pants.

Wyoming. Could he get *more* different than Ohio? He'd left the lush greens of Oberlin right after graduation. Kissed Penny goodbye—nothing serious so no heartache —and headed west.

"Surfing?" She was an overachiever type and was joining the Peace Corps, headed for Africa with her honors degree in psychology.

"Sure. Get me some sun and surf."

"And surfer babes?" Penny didn't sound even a little hurt, which meant their time together had been less meaningful than he'd thought. *Chump!*

"Sure, why not? What else am I supposed to do with a degree in French Literature?" He suspected that the defensive tone hadn't served him well.

"Have you ever surfed?"

"Now's my big chance."

"That's a pretty directionless choice, Mac." She'd shaken her head sadly, her Farrah Fawcett blonde curls wafting about her face. She was as fun as she was trendy and cute. They'd only been together for the last couple months of senior year though, now that he thought about it, she'd always given him the feeling that she was slumming a bit and mostly marking time.

He'd never been one for high goals. His dad had been a professor of French Lit at Loyola until he'd stroked out (in two ways) in a coed's arms at forty-eight. Mac had decided to follow in his footsteps, for reasons passing anyone's understanding—including his own. Even more disillusioning, he'd generally had better luck with the French Lit than the coeds. Penny had been the exception, not the rule. But even if he applied for the Peace Corps now, they'd be all out of sync. Not that he wanted to.

Wanted to.

For four years everyone—the entire college experience —had gone on and on about how they could all be anything they "wanted to." But for the life of him he couldn't figure out what that might be for him.

Travolta's "Oo-oo-oo" croon with perky blonde Newton-John gave way to ABBA's *Take a Chance on Me.*

The job recruiters had taken one look at his long hair, his mastery of Middle French literature, and his liberal arts school attitude, then looked the other way. No chance on him. *Oo-oo-oo!* Surfing was still the best bet he'd heard in a while. He'd delayed with some buddies who had a cabin on Lake Michigan—to work on building up some swimmer muscles, or maybe to have one last collegiate-style beer blast—and a week with his mom in Chicago. But it reached late July and he was missing summer in the surf. That had finally gotten him heading west again.

He pulled off in Cheyenne to study his road atlas as he chowed down on a Burger King Double Whopper and fries. Straight west or time to turn south? Holding west for Salt Lake could be a thing, not that he wanted to hang there, but it would be something to see. Or cut down to Denver then climb the Rockies. His Mazda pickup had been making some funny noises lately, so maybe the Rockies wasn't the best idea. Of course breaking down in the vast emptiness of Wyoming…

Turning the key, *Rocky Mountain High* blared out of the radio. Must be a Top Ten of the Past thing, but he'd take it as an omen. Denver it was. The randomness of his directionless life lived on.

Then he twisted the ignition the rest of the way and got that nasty ratcheting sound he'd heard lately. Except this time the engine didn't start. Again. No luck.

A cowboy, complete with boots and a big old hat, strolling by with his own burger bag, stopped and listened. "Yep! You got a cooked starter solenoid. Jason there can fix you up." He hooked a thumb at a service station across the street. "Need a push?"

Ten minutes later he was officially stuck in Cheyenne, Wyoming while they waited for parts. "Have it for you in the morning."

"C'mon, kid." Jason couldn't be more than a couple years older. "See how real people live." And he'd followed the cowboy back to his truck which was big enough he could have parked his Mazda in the back of it...if the starter had worked.

CHAPTER 2

A ma reluctantly followed her mother into the dance ring at Indian Village. The circle of white teepees had been erected for Cheyenne Frontier Days, just as it had for the last eighty years. Ten days every year that were the bane of her existence. Even private, tribal powwows boasted more RVs than teepees these days, but the truth didn't mix well with the stereotypes in people's heads. And RVs definitely weren't as photogenic as the line of white teepees on the Cheyenne prairie.

There were cowboys and farmers in the crowd, but there were far more tourists whose beer bellies conflicted badly with the newer, tighter fashions. Some women gave in to the mid-summer's heat with strapless tops, but many still had jackets so that they could wear their shoulder pads. The crowd sat or stood five deep between the circle of teepees and the grassy dance field.

Come for the show. Come see the redskin girl dance a blessing to the day—an importance you will never understand.

After me, watch my cousin the hoop dancer. A great tradition tracing all of the way back to Tony White Cloud performing it in the Lucille Ball movie Valley of the Sun. *Yes, come see the least authentic powwow dance you can imagine, up next.*

Yet Ama knew better than to ever say or show such a thing. She was the good daughter. The youngest lead dancer since Great-grandmother Swooping Bird. Her mother's scowl and her father's disdain were for her brother, never for Ama. Like the water that was her name, she flowed around problems, always quiet and level.

Watch me dance. I know every step perfectly. Not the modern ones, but the way that has been handed down directly by Great-grandmother from her great-grandmother. Leave this world for a moment and see how we tread the Great Plains when they still belonged to the Cheyenne, Crow, and Pawnee.

She let her vision unfocus as she found the rhythm of the drums and her feet hit the soil in traditionally short, hard steps. But it wasn't the shaking of the drums that called to her in the dance, it was the *tahpeno*—the cedar courtship flute. She'd never been able to resist its call and she could feel it capture her arms and let her float.

See the flight of the tiniest hummingbird greet the opening of the morning flowers in my fingers. Follow the robin and the dove in my hands. See the great eagle soar in my arms high above the family ranch. And watch the swallow swoop and play at dusk in how I float.

The tourists didn't matter.

The other dancers faded aside.

It was just the flute's call, the cycle of this day's bird-flight, and her dance.

In this moment, for this one precious instant, it felt as

if she balanced between two worlds. Her life as a paralegal for a divorce lawyer had nothing to do with this dance, except when she was immersed in it, then it was the whole rest of her life that lost meaning.

As the swallow returned to her evening nest and the dance came to a close, the path of her feet—still stomping to the unceasing, unceasing rhythm of the drums—led her close to the crowd.

As Henry Morning Crow's flute ended the day with the first call of the *mista*—the great horned owl, the spirit of the night, *hoo-h'Hoo hoo hoo*—Ama came back into her own body. She planted her feet with the last beat of the drum and looked once more through her own eyes rather than the birds'.

The crowd's roar of approval and applause was, as ever, a harsh shock. She could never grow used to it. It was from the wrong world: not herself or the dance, not her tribe. Instead it battered at her, hard and forceful.

A man stood directly in front of where her dance had led her. A man acting like no other in the crowd. He did not applaud; he did not even appear to breathe.

His looks didn't blend into the crowd either. He was her age and lean with strong shoulders; the sort of man who would never need shoulder pads. His collar-long hair, as dark as her own, framed his fair face. It was a good face, a strong one. His eyes were steel gray and seemed to see past the costume and the dancer. She knew her looks were a throwback to Swooping Bird, who had often been declared the most beautiful Cheyenne of her generation. But he didn't seem to see that either.

Men always saw her dancing or her beauty. Her

parents saw the good girl. Her tribe viewed her as the granddaughter of a great Peace Chief and the great-granddaughter of a still celebrated dancer.

It was as if this man could see her as no one except the mirror ever had. As herself.

CHAPTER 3

M ac lay on his longboard, letting the swells roll
beneath him. The chilly Pacific Ocean was actually pacific for a change. The waves had settled an hour
ago and he was content to simply lie in the sun and wait
as he was lifted and lowered by their lazy rhythm. This
had become his favorite part of surfing. He could stand up
and ride a wave now, but he doubted he'd ever be good.

"There they are again," Ama spoke lazily from the
board beside him. She wasn't any better at surfing than he
was, but at least she was far better looking while doing it.
Also, her dancer's grace always looked so elegant that her
lack of skill mattered far less than his own clumsy efforts.
Her hair, a straight slash to her waist, now lay over the
back of her wetsuit like a soft blanket. Her suit was the
same sky blue as the deer hide dress she'd worn at the
Frontier Days dance. Out of the wetsuit when ashore, the
pure white bikini she favored highlighted her dark skin—
and completely scrambled his hormones. She'd taken to

wearing dark sunglasses which only added to her mystery.

He was still unsure why she'd joined him for the drive to California. She hadn't volunteered her reasons and he'd been afraid to ask. For two months he'd had the most astonishing lover of his life in their little beach shack. They weren't broke, not yet, but this couldn't last and *that* troubled him. Unlike Penny, he'd be majorly bummed when Ama Dances Like Water left to return to her tribe. She'd given no hint of such a plan, but it worried him anyway.

September had seen the summer surfers retreat except on the weekends. Only the hardcore beach bums still remained afloat under the mid-October sun.

Ama didn't speak often, so when she did, he always paid attention. He followed the direction of her gaze.

Coronado Beach was no longer hazed by the heat as it had been since their arrival, but it was no less bright beneath the midday sun.

Mac propped his chin on his hands and squinted against the glare.

Navy SEALs. Only twenty remained in the group of men in green. There had been at least a hundred the first time they ran on the beach a month ago. They never ran where it was easy, down by the waves. Instead, they were always up on the dry beach where the heat burned and every step slipped and dragged in the deep sand. They sang as they ran. Four trainers ran with them. He'd seen the trainers haranguing their every step as their numbers dwindled—the sharp clang of a bell marking another grunt "ringing out" and quitting because he couldn't make the grade.

Today was different. Today the trainers sang with the running recruits. A team. Those who remained were becoming a team. In perfect unison, immensely fit, and dependent on one another.

He lay his head once more on his hands and contemplated the woman stretched beside him, rising and falling on the swells of the Pacific Ocean.

What would it take to make Ama *not* flow away from him? To not dismiss him with an easy shrug as Penny had. That struck him as being of desperate importance. Perhaps the first such thing in his entire life.

Had she pointed out the SEAL team for a reason? He had to think about that.

Ama could only stare at Mac in surprise.

He had transformed past recognition without changing at all. Not a caterpillar turned into a butterfly, but rather a man transformed into a Man.

He was so much stronger now than even the surfing had made him; the physical power of his embrace utterly breathtaking in many ways.

But his eyes still saw her with Eagle's vision and he heard her with Coyote's sharp ears. Being with Mac had made her feel closer to her tribe and her heritage than she ever had back in Wyoming. He'd insisted that she return to the next Cheyenne Frontier Days to dance, and he'd been right. It was an important glimpse of her culture that she'd nearly lost all sight of in San Diego.

Over this year, his gentleness had faded, except towards her. In that he was as unvarying as the Great Spirit itself.

Living on the inside of his world, she could see how

different he had become to the outside world. Mac had pulled on a shroud of power like a dancer who pulled the skin of Buffalo over his head and transformed into the beast.

All in white, Mac's uniform shone as brightly as the sun. And like a piece ripped from the sun itself, the golden SEAL trident shone fresh and new upon his left breast.

Other graduates of the year-long course were surrounded by their families or wives.

She found herself reluctant to walk up to Mac. He was so transformed that she half wondered if she still belonged in his world. Her dance had led her to stand in front of him. But had his dance of becoming a Navy SEAL led him toward her?

He often joked that he didn't believe in such things as something guiding her steps, but she'd had no other way to explain it. He *did* say often that "he wasn't complaining about the results."

And now?

He strode up to her, so tall and beautiful in his rugged way.

Then, without hesitation, not looking to see who of his new SEAL brothers were watching, he went down on bent knee before her. The silence rushed outward through the celebrating SEALs faster than a wave breaking on a reef until all attention was focused upon them.

"Now, am I finally worthy of you?" His words were so soft.

"Since the day my dance led me to you." And she must

be worthy of him for he had come to her and that was all that mattered. For though he often said that he would be less of a man without her, she knew that she would also be less of a woman without her Mac.

Mac lay face down and wondered if he'd ever breathe again. The heat drove into his body a thousand times hotter than any mere splash of the San Diego sunshine. Hotter even than Ama could still make his blood race after thirteen years together.

Why was it now, when they were ten thousand miles away that he could think of nothing but his wife and twelve-year old son? Ama had given him the gift of a son. It focused his thoughts. Even lying face down in the burning sand, so desperate that he wanted to give up or wither away, he knew one thing was true. Only by serving with honor and completing the mission could he face them. They were his strength and he needed to be theirs.

The dust of the Iraqi soil clogged every pore. Fifty kilometers behind Saddam's lines, his four-SEAL squad lay unmoving, covered in the sand, waiting out the midday heat.

Elements of the Iraqi Republican Guard were patrolling the area. A full platoon—ten times their number—and a pair of tanks. A T-72's treads had missed their hiding position by less than five feet, but if they'd so much as flinched, they'd have been gunned down before they could even raise a weapon. So they'd waited—and been lucky.

The Guard and their tanks weren't the real target. The targets were the Scud missiles they guarded. The ones that Saddam was firing at Israel and Saudi Arabia. The start of Operation Desert Storm was delayed for a week while Special Ops hunted and killed the Scud sites. The ones along the Jordanian border to the west and aimed at Israel were being hunted by Delta and SAS, but his SEAL team had been lucky enough to draw the short straw on the wasteland between Kuwait and Nasiriyah in the southeast corner of the country.

Lying low through the day, they'd gathered valuable intel, including talk of the three other sites hidden in the area. It was finally falling dusk. Come full dark, they'd pull back and pinpoint those other three—calling in simultaneous airstrikes against all four launchers.

This one—

Barty grunted.

"Al'ama!" A mild epithet by Arabic's typically porno-graphic curse standards. A Republican Guard, stepping off the path to piss, had stumbled on Barty Hughes —literally.

The guard struggled to keep his sidearm steady while grabbing for his rapidly sagging pants. He had Barty square in his sights. The hammer was already on the move.

Mac emerged from his hiding place just a step to the

guard's other side. No other RGs nearby at the moment, but that wouldn't last.

He came up out of the sand with his KA-BAR knife already out of its leg sheath. Before the guard could react, Mac had rammed seven inches of steel upward through the guard's chin. With a twist, he sliced his brain's connection to the rest of his nervous system.

Just like the Vietnam vets who trained him had promised, the man's body shut down all at once without a single sound. His other teammates emerged from the sand.

He dragged the corpse—with the knife still in place to minimize blood flow onto the sand—back out of sight behind a thorn bush.

"Make a hole."

The other three scrabbled quickly in the sand. When it was a foot deep, he twisted the corpse around and flopped it in, yanking free his blade.

He watched while they covered it back up. It wouldn't hide him for long, but it didn't have to. By midnight, this site would be blasted to smithereens.

Night had fallen with a desert's abruptness and they faded away.

"Thanks, bro." Barty slapped him on the shoulder as they moved out.

It was the first real action either of them had seen. The '80s had been more about training and humanitarian missions. This whole Desert Shield / Desert Storm thing was new even to a SEAL with a decade in the teams.

"You get my back next time." But he couldn't find it in

him to thump Barty back as they jogged off into the dark to find and pinpoint the next site.

He'd signed up for this and trained for it, but he'd never killed a man before. He'd *seen* death. Almost died himself during the disaster which was Desert One—the US' attempt to free the hostages from Iran in 1980 had ended in a fiery disaster. But he'd never dealt it before.

The next time he touched Ama, would he feel the mark on his hand? Would she?

Maybe.

But for the first time he finally understood just how fast a man's life could end. His own life as well. But he had a wife *and* a son.

As they ran through the darkness, he knew he was at a fork in the path. A decision. Did killing one man count as his lifetime quota and, if so, that would lead him back to… where? To their small house in San Diego? To surfing and bobbing on the waves without a purpose?

No. He wouldn't allow the death of an enemy to change the path of his life. He now understood what Ama had once said, that life's changes must come from the good, not the bad. *Let the Good be our guide.*

Ama had changed more than his life, she'd changed his world. And she'd given him a son who had had changed his heart.

He thumped his fist against Barty's shoulder as they ran side-by-side. Barty wasn't the only one who was thankful to be alive. Mac would stay in the SEALs. He would fight to keep his family safe despite the danger.

At least until he found the next fork in the path formed from joy, not death.

CHAPTER 6

Ama rode behind her beloved men. She had grown up riding horses, a skill she had almost forgotten but her body had remembered as easily as any dance. The two of them rode miserably, yet acted as if falling off would be the greatest possible wound to their manly pride. She was careful to reserve her smile for when they were looking the other way.

How had her life led her to riding across this lush prairie ranch while listening to her husband's and son's hearty voices, loudly reassuring themselves of their competence? How had her life led to any of the places it had?

She had followed a young boy with mystical eyes to San Diego against her parents' wishes. They had lived together on the beach as well as overseas when his assignments allowed. The nights apart she had slept curled around the phone, praying that each time it rang, it would be his voice on the other end of the line and not his commander's. For twenty years her prayers had been answered.

For twenty years she had worn the warrior's face each time he left—assured and proud. Each time he returned, she'd worn the wife's—thankful to the Maheo Sky Chief or any other power that might be listening for his safe return. And she had done her very best to hide her tears from Mark on all the nights between.

She looked at the open prairie beneath the vast blue sky. They were safe now, in this instant: her husband returned from war and her son not yet gone. This ranch had been another family's dream, and it was clear that they had struggled before they left. It would take a lot of work to bring the ranch back to life. But she'd never feared hard work and a SEAL knew of no other kind. It could be a home. Perhaps the one she'd always dreamed of.

Mac's dream had come complete the day he retired. His entire team had stood down together—those who had retired before twenty years had come to the celebration on the beach at Coronado. They had raised a glass to those who had fallen. The SEALs all agreed they'd been fortunate that so few of their teammates had died, but she had felt battered anew by each name that was called in that toast.

Later in the party, after her nerves had finally calmed down, Mac had taken her hand. Just as he had twenty years before, he'd gone down on one knee before all his SEAL brothers. There had been laughter among the team at the memory.

She had waited to see what he would ask this time.

"You have dreamed *my* dream long enough, my love. I think I found a way to help dream *your* dream now."

So she and Mark, who had come to the retirement party on a school break from West Point, had followed him here to this ranch nestled close against the feet of the towering Front Range.

Up to Wyoming. Past Cheyenne where she'd returned every summer to see family and to dance. North of Yellowstone and into the heart of Montana where the grasslands were alive with the yellow and purple of summer flowers.

She patted her horse on the neck and watched her two men riding beneath the shimmering blue sky. They were so excited with dreams of building a new home here, even if neither one had much of an idea about what that meant. Neither of them had ever lived in the country. She was shocked that they had yet to fall off their horses—though there had been many close calls.

But this was a dream *she* understood.

Mac had passed that certainty, that perfect clarity of self on to his son. A senior at West Point, he stood as tall and handsome as his father. His dark hair short for the training, had run long through the sunlit years of his teens—just as his father's had when Ama had first seen him. Mark's skin was closer to her tone than Mac's; his face so handsome he could have been one of the Cheyenne. Except for the eyes. He had his father's blue-gray eyes—soft when he was happy and like cold steel when angered.

They'd ridden deep into the ranch on horses borrowed from a neighboring cattle rancher. At a river that wound through the miles of Montana pastureland, she had taught them how to fish. They had planned on two days, yet stayed for a week, living off what they caught. She had snared a rabbit, pleased that she remembered the tricks to skin it and cook it over a campfire—lessons learned from her father so long ago.

Now they were returning. Across the rolling hills, they had climbed the high bluff that sheltered the main ranch buildings. A mile down the dirt road, the cattle ranch where their horses belonged could just be seen. The horses were anxious for their stables, but Mac and Mark were finally confident enough in the saddle to at least keep them from running off. That still didn't mean they knew anything about ranch life.

"Put up a new barn there," Mac pointed to a swale in the land that would be wet in autumn's rainfall, "and you could start a nice herd of cattle."

But it would be a fine place for a swimming hole with only a little work. Besides, cattle were smelly, rude, and not very rewarding to the rancher. She'd seen many of her father's friends broken by a bad season, a runaway disease, even rustlers.

"Sure," Mark had agreed with his father. "And build a bunkhouse for the hands up here on the bluff so they get a nice view. Treat your team well and they'll treat you well."

This place where the harsh north winds would run chill across the Canadian Plains and slam straight into them all winter.

There was a reason that the old ranch house down below had been built on the south side of the bluff. Ten years abandoned, it still stood square and strong with a long porch wrapping around three sides. Thirty miles to the nearest town, it had not been plagued by vandals and the weather had claimed only two windows.

Halfway between their perch on the bluff and the big house were several copses of Ponderosa pines. Sheltered from the north, their view was to the southeast, not of the ranch, but rather the neighbor's land that seemed to roll to the horizon. It had made the view of the mountains once over the bluff a surprise and a gift.

A few weathered cabins still huddled among the pines. A little clearing, a little fixing, and guests could come there. Their future happy voices seemed to catch on the breeze that washed over the tall grass much as the waves had when she would watch Mac just to see what he would do next.

The old horse barn and the ranch manager's house still stood strong as well.

She had lived so much of her life alone. First, with a tribe she had felt curiously disconnected from. Later, separated during tour after tour from the one man who had ever made her heart soar like the dance. And finally, after her son had gone to West Point to become the man his father was, she'd been completely alone. The last three years had been a time of holding her heart closed and waiting.

Well, that was done and she wouldn't miss it. Her heart could open now and soar like an eagle. She stretched her fingers out and let them feel the breeze trickling between them.

There would be people here, and laughter. She could already see them: riding horses, fishing in the streams, and eating good camp fare at the long wooden table they'd discovered still standing in the ranch house dining room. Mac could lead hunting parties or teach shooting on a range (over the other side of the rise so that guests didn't have to hear it). People would come here to escape, to discover happiness. It could work.

This Montana ranch wouldn't be just some step woven into the old, she decided. It would be a whole new dance.

CHAPTER 7

Mac kept an eye on Ama as they rode down the hill, past the big house, and along the dirt driveway.

He tried to read what she was thinking about the place. The verdict looked hopeful, but she'd always been hard to read. He was fairly sure he had it right, because when she was feeling deepest was when she was quietest. And she'd barely said a word since they'd left the high bluff lookout.

Even back at the retirement party, he'd been watching for her reaction but been unable to read it. Barty and his dad had approached Mac with an idea.

What to do after retirement had worried at him. A SEAL knew how to fight. A SEAL knew that nothing could stop him once he had a mission. Except, in retiring, Mac no longer *had* a mission.

"Thanks again for saving my boy's life," Bart Sr. had handed him a fresh beer.

"Served twenty years on the same team, seemed like

the right thing to do," Mac had earned a laugh from them both.

Bart Sr. had been a Marine in Vietnam and understood. Barty had saved Mac's life a time or two as well over the years—though not so graphically. That's just how it worked on the teams.

"Got a place up in Montana," Bart had told him, while looking off into the distance over Coronado Beach and the Pacific. "Twenty thousand acres of the prettiest land you've ever laid eyes on. Former owners moved on a decade ago and I grabbed it. Needs tending."

Mac could only shake his head. "I saved some. Ama's good with money and I sent home all I could, but we can't afford a ranch."

"Not talking about selling it to you. If you'd like, it's yours and your kin's for as long as you tend it. When you're done, I'll buy it back for the cost of improvements. No risk. Go up there and take the family. Once you give it a good look over, I know you'll love it. All yours if you want it. Did I mention that I'm right grateful you saved my son's life?"

"Might have," Mac had agreed as he had looked over at Ama standing with a few of the other SEALs. People were drawn to her, but "social" wasn't how he ever thought of her. Ama and city life had never made sense. Not in Cheyenne. Not in San Diego. Not outside the Marine Corps base in Böblingen, Germany.

There were images, moments, that had pulled him through the worst of Hell Week when half the remaining hopefuls had rung out and quit because they couldn't hack it. Grown men, tough soldiers, had openly wept at their failure. But each time he'd had to dig deep, there were certain memories that had let him find the resolve to stick out the training or to survive when by all rights he should have died in some foreign hole.

He always remembered her lost in the dance—the tall beauty in sky-blue deer hide dress and boots. And he always remembered her floating out on that surfboard when the waves were too quiet to ride but too peaceful to leave. She belonged somewhere she could find that peace.

Bart's description had sounded completely on the mark. So completely that Mac had asked him to arrange one other favor. Once he'd asked, Bart had slapped him on the back as if they'd been comrades in the same war instead of thirty years apart on opposite sides of the world.

But now, here in Montana, it was only Ama's opinion that mattered and, as ever, she kept her thoughts carefully to herself.

His family rode three abreast down the ranch's drive. Looking ahead, he saw that the broken arch of the ranch sign had been replaced while they'd been camped back along the river. New and hopefully carved just as he'd asked of Bart. Mac truly hoped that he'd made the right decision in asking his favor.

The cattle rancher's daughter—a blonde sprite who couldn't be more than ten—galloped across the field toward them as if riding was more natural than breathing. She reached them just as they arrived beneath the sign, its message facing out toward the world.

"Would you like a picture? Pa said he thought you might like a picture." She flourished a Polaroid camera at them. "Saw you up on the bluff looking around and I guessed when you'd get down here. Guessed dead right." She was breathless with her own success.

Ama's nod was all Mac needed. He had no photo of her dancing. Nor of her long body in a sleek wetsuit afloat on the Pacific Ocean. But this time he would. His whole family at once, gathered under the arch of the repaired ranch sign.

Julie, that was the sprite's name, got them all lined up on their horses, then backed her own horse up without touching the reins as she peered through the finder.

"Whoa," she called softly and the horse whoaed. Maybe he'd have to hire her to give him lessons. Ama, of course, rode a horse even more elegantly than she'd ridden those long ago waves.

Julie snapped it and the square print churned out the front slot.

"Take another," he called to her.

She eyed him over the camera.

"Dollar apiece," he offered.

"Two for five dollars. I'm saving up for an entry in the junior rodeo at the fair." Not greedy, just ambitious. Something a SEAL always appreciated.

He couldn't help smiling and nodded for her to fire away.

She did, then walked the horse back up to him, flapping a photo in each hand as they developed while the camera dangled around her neck. He solemnly fished out a five and traded it for the two photos.

"Don't tell my dad," Julie folded the bill very small then tucked it deep into a jeans pocket. She grabbed her reins, spun about, and galloped off with her long blonde hair floating behind her.

Mac handed one of the photos to Mark. "Your copy, son. This is family. Keep it close." Mark's nod said that he understood, or thought he did. For now it was enough, he'd learn the rest when luck and love found him.

"Say, Dad," Mark had raised his sunglasses to inspect the photo as it developed. "It's a cool sign, but…"

Mac glanced at the photo he still held as Ama rode forward enough to look back and see the sign itself.

"Looks good to me, Mark. Let's see what your mom thinks."

If Ama had been quiet before, she'd now gone so perfectly still that she might as well be hypnotized by the arcing sign of new wood.

"It spells Henderson's Ranch," Mark continued, just a little bit oblivious to what was really going on. "Which is great. And I think you and Mom will love it here. But shouldn't it be plural with the apostrophe after the s, not before?"

But Mac was still waiting for Ama's final reaction.

She slowly lowered her eyes to look at him.

Just like that long ago day at the end of her dance. She had looked at him and a smile had slowly bloomed to life across her lovely features. Love at first sight was far too slow a word for her effect on him.

Until now, she had always lived his life. And it had been a good one.

Now he expected that he would be even more content living hers.

"It's *her* dream now, son. Her ranch. I can only hope

you find a woman who makes you feel like I'm feeling right now."

Then he managed to nudge the horse forward until he could kiss his wife. They'd make a home together under the brilliant blue arch of Montana's Big Sky.

EMILY'S CHRISTMAS GIFT

When Christmas is not all it seems, maybe the best gift of all isn't under the tree.

Major Emily Beale (retired—mostly) keeps her hand in the Black Ops world remotely from the family horse ranch on Montana's Front Range. Her husband, Major Mark Henderson (fully retired), has settled comfortably into his new role as father and ranch operator.

Years ago, she helped rescue a young girl. But when Emily's childhood friend, the former President of the United States, comes to visit, he raises doubts about the girl's safety. No longer so sure of herself, Emily must reach deep into the White House's secret library to find the answers. Little does she know the true location of Emily's Christmas Gift.

INTRODUCTION TO THIS STORY

Henderson's Ranch was rapidly becoming a haven for military veterans, each finding their own form of peace and true love.

Emily Beale, who had helped her husband find and accept his role out of the military, had always shown a perfect acceptance of the changes to her own life.

Except that wasn't the Emily Beale who had launched so many books, series, and short stories. The military had been her life and I could feel that it wasn't something she could possibly give up that easily.

She had her background role as the hidden voice behind the *White House Protection Force* series. But that was for the military soldier.

What about for the woman?

So, I went looking and remembered the first Christmas I spent with my new family over two decades ago. I remember the moment of magic, lifting my new six-year old kid aloft to complete the tree.

And I found this story.

CHAPTER 1

E mily watched Mark being as calm as could be and tried not to resent it. When the heavy Montana snowstorms of December kept them indoors at the main ranch house, he was content to slouch low on the couch and watch a Disney movie with the girls in the cozy family area off the kitchen.

If they wanted to build a fort—Emily always thought of it as a fort, though the girls kept insisting they were tents—Mark would reconfigure the family sitting area off the kitchen no matter what inconvenience it caused the adults.

Between the three of them, they made sure that each construction looked unlike any prior effort. A tropical paradise one time, decorated mostly with one of the ranch hand's awful Hawaiian shirt collection. Another time, a Cheyenne teepee built with Mark's mother's lovely weavings. She'd particularly liked that one. Being in Montana, and especially if Julie was around to help,

Western themes were common, often with horse tack or some of her rodeo trophies for decoration.

In the summers Mark lived to fly tourists around in his helicopter and fish, but in the winter his one joy was keeping his girls happy.

That she herself was one of "his girls" always made their daughters giggle with delight. And she *was* happy. All she had to do was watch her daughters and she let their constantly bubbling joy wash over her. They might build their forts—*tents* with their father. But it was never considered complete until she had joined them for the final tour. Mark often left some final task for her to do so that she'd at least feel included. Then they would all lie in it together—Mark at the center with all three of "his girls" clinging happily to him.

Those were the best moments of her life. Perhaps a close second to waking in his arms on the long quiet winter mornings before Tessa and Belle sprang to life like a pair of Jill-in-the-boxes.

She'd known he was a good man and a great commander, but his daughters had never met "The Viper" who used to scare the shit out of everybody, including her. His steel gray eyes had rarely been revealed from behind his mirrored shades. He'd even proposed to her while wearing them—after dark. Which was perhaps the only thing that had kept her from turning into a complete empty-headed mush in that moment.

But his daughters only saw the sky gray that his eyes shone when he was happiest—and the mirrored shades were now worn only in the strong Montana sun. It was impossible for her *not* be happy while she watched the stern, taciturn, demanding Major Mark "The Viper" Henderson (retired) have no compunction about acting as the total goofball with his girls. He was a better father than she was a mother, but she didn't know what to do about that. When they were upset, it was her they came to, so she still had something. But it often meant she got the tears and Mark earned all the cheers.

Emily didn't resent it…much. She mostly just wished it was somehow different.

She turned to the fire and watched what she could see of the flames. They were partially blocked by a great bulge in this week's fort, which was huge by any previous standard.

This room was where the family lived during the day when they weren't out on the ranch. The high-timbered main room and the dining room with its forty-person pine table was for the guests. In the long, bitter, off-season months, it was also where all the locals gathered for the occasional party to break the monotony of winter.

That was for others. The family lived in the kitchen. The kitchen itself was a full commercial setup, decorated like in ranch-house warm timber and cool granite stone. At the near end stood a large plank table of Douglas fir where the family and the ranch hands ate their meals together.

This sitting area to the side had a big stone fireplace, and a scattering of couches and armchairs enough for the entire staff…or there had been until the kids started showing up. Once they graduated from lap-sized, they would have to squeeze in some more furniture. The bookcases that lined the river stone walls already had more shelves added to accommodate the girls' picture books.

Of course more furniture couldn't happen with their latest fort in place—she could only see half the fire from her favorite end of the couch.

It was like a mighty Christmas igloo, its walls built high with pillows raided from all of the guest cabins that were closed for the winter. Mark had waded out into the freezing dawn this morning to cut down and drag home a ten-foot larch to stand at its center. Now, with the tree up and their pillow-wall built, the three of them were madly working away inside. Only the tree's single uppermost branch was visible above the domed roof, like a wide smoke hole escaping the dome of pillows.

Whenever there was a newborn about, either Chelsea's or Julie's boy, their father was instantly abandoned without further thought—which made her feel a little better. Of course, then Emily had to keep a close eye so that the girls didn't smother the two infants with affection. How in the world she'd raised two such…*girls* was a mystery to her. At five, Tessa was an utter extrovert who had all the ranch hands completely wrapped around her tiny pinkie. Belle at three was the steadier one, but only by comparison.

Emily didn't pace when the heavy snow and the biting cold winds forced them to remain indoors, but she wished she'd taken up watching sports on television or something. But after a career of flying helicopters first to war and then to wildfire, watching a bunch of guys chase a football up and down a chunk of AstroTurf in little one- and two-yard spurts couldn't be called exciting.

"I'm absolutely hiring Mark for the next seventeen years," Chelsea plummeted down into the big armchair beside Emily's end of the couch, then had to drag her fingers through her long hair to toss it over her shoulder so she could see. Her cheeks were brilliant red after crossing the snow from where she and her husband, the ranch manager, lived on the other side of the barnyard. Maybe Emily should grow her gold-blonde hair as long, the way Mark kept hinting, but it had been chopped dead straight to her shoulders for her entire life.

Emily saw Mark now sitting on the braided rug with Chelsea's three-month old boy Christopher cradled in his arms—whose hair was already as red as his mother's. Tessa and Belle were leaning on his thighs from either side and reaching over to inspect the infant who watched with such wide, serious eyes. Her own fair hair hadn't been passed on to either daughter, having no chance against Mark's genes from his brown-haired father and Cheyenne mother.

"Or maybe I'll just knock you off and get two husbands, keep Doug for me and have Mark for the kid." Chelsea extended her feet toward the fire.

"I'm notoriously hard to kill." Emily's specialty had been black-in-black missions. Black ops so sensitive that they were talked about with no one, ever. And so dangerous that each one was a curse of its own. Mark accompanied her on or referred vaguely to four—she'd stopped counting as she neared ten.

"Oh, don't worry, Emily," Chelsea slouched lower. "I'd like, uh, get Julie to do it for me. She was raised a cowgirl and knows how to do the icky stuff."

"I'm a horsegirl now. And do what?" Julie settled very slowly on the couch beside Emily, careful not to wake Jared asleep in her arms. Like her own children, Jared had his father's dark hair and eyes rather than Julia's wheat blonde and blue. If he'd slept through the snowy trek down the hill from their cabin, then it would take far more than a small bump to wake him, but Emily knew better than to say such a thing to a new mother. She had to smile at her own worries about Tessa in the beginning.

She did scoop up Jared and hold him while Julie shed her thick coat and tossed it over a maple wood chair. Then she settled back on the plaid sofa and took Jared back, again with infinite care.

Like the toddler-magnets they were, Tessa and Belle appeared on either side of Julie. Tessa sat on Julie's far side, but Belle pushed and squirmed—with plenty of bumps that Jared never noticed—until she was sitting between Emily and Julie. Emily looped an arm around her daughter, not as if there was anywhere else to put it, and kissed her on top of the head.

"I need you to...uh," Chelsea glanced at the two young girls before answering Julie, "...*remove* Emily for me. Kinda permanently so I can have Mark as a full-time babysitter."

"Too late," Julie gently blocked Belle reaching over to wake Jared. Belle was completely enamored of Jared's big eyes and the two of them could stare at each other for hours. "I've already got dibs. Besides, I thought we liked Emily?"

"We do. But where has that gotten us?"

"They grow, you know," Emily decided it was time for

a subject change to something other than her demise. "Far too quickly, I might add." She pulled one of Ama's Cheyenne blankets off the back of the couch—this one she'd loved from the first moment, so rich with warm golds and dark reds in a geometric pattern. Spreading it over Julie's and the girls' laps earned her contented smiles.

"See?" Julie looked over at Chelsea. "She knows things. I vote that we keep her."

"Well, she is out there ahead of us," Chelsea finally agreed. "So, what are the good bits waiting for us?"

"We're almost done with diapers."

"Oh God," the two women moaned in unison. "Can't happen too soon."

"Thankfully, Mark is okay trading off on that duty."

"That does it," Chelsea declared. "Sorry, Emily. We really like you, but you're *totally* toast."

"I've still got dibs on Mark." The threat didn't seem too serious as Julie was looking down at her sleeping son with a big smile on her face.

Mark was bent halfway over from placing the now-sleeping Christopher into Chelsea's arms when he finally clued into the last comment. He paused, inspecting all of them carefully.

"Why does this sound like a conversation I want no part of?"

"Because you are a very smart man who loves his wife above any other woman on Earth."

"It's true," Mark shrugged happily before stepping around the back of the couch and leaning down to kiss her from the side.

Emily could feel her internal compass slowly

returning to True North. It wasn't often she flew off course, but with Mark's lips on hers, she managed to rediscover her rudder control.

"Oh man," Chelsea groaned in envy.

"Chelsea's right," Julie agreed. "You'd better watch your back, Emily. We're ganging up on you and you're going down. Soon."

"By Christmas."

Emily ignored them both as Mark drew out the kiss to tease them. No complaints from her.

"Where are *your* men?" Mark asked when he finally let her surface for air, leaving her heartrate up about Black Hawk rotor speed. "Two such beautiful women with babies in their arms shouldn't be sitting here unkissed."

"They abandoned us."

"Left us destitute."

"They may have mumbled something about feeding the horses."

"So here we sit."

"In our prime."

"Unkissed," they finished in unison and both aimed ridiculous puckers at Mark and batted their eyelashes. Well, Chelsea did. Julie tried but mostly looked down and blushed for being so forward.

"Feeding the horses, huh? I'd better go check on them." He didn't leave at a run, but he definitely used his best ground-eating stride.

"Ooo," Chelsea cooed loudly. "Looks good from behind too. All mine."

Mark double-timed it out as the three of them shared a laugh.

When he was gone, there was a long silence. Long enough for Belle to slip into a nap against Emily's side and for Tessa to yawn broadly before curling up at the end of the sofa and resting her head on Julie's thigh while Jared wrapped his tiny hand around her pinkie without quite waking.

"What's up with you, Emily?" Julie asked softly.

"There's something up with you?" Chelsea peered at her in surprise.

"Nothing." Emily ignored the slump that Mark had only temporarily lifted. She toyed with the blanket's fringe for a moment before she caught herself at it and tucked her hands out of sight. "Besides, since when can either of you tell what I'm thinking?"

"Since forever. We're your best friends," Julie spoke softly.

"Yeah. Maybe we aren't all experienced and old like you, but we know shit."

They'd both found the love of their life and repro-duced in their early twenties. It had taken her until thirty to find love, then more years of service, finally the first kid…and that had been five years ago. Forty wasn't here yet, but it was incoming—fast. She closed her eyes. This was December. She'd been born in… Yep, really fast.

"Is forty bumming you out?"

Emily sat with it for a while. "No, I don't think that's it…"

"Told you something was up with her," Julie whispered to Chelsea.

"Of course, you two youngsters are enough to make a grown woman a little nuts."

"But you love us both anyway, huh?"

Emily looked at Chelsea and couldn't deny that truth.

"Like daughters?" Julie's voice was slightly wistful. Her family life hadn't been real fun. Just the hard life of a cattle ranch with a strict father, a silent mother, and three older brothers, but none of the joy she'd discovered when she'd fallen in love with the man who was now Henderson's Ranch's head chef.

"*Daughters?*" Emily winced. "Now you're just *trying* to make me feel old. How about younger sisters?"

Julie actually nodded fiercely. As if it was important.

Chelsea too was blinking hard. "If I wasn't afraid of waking this little terror, I'd come over there and give you major kiss."

Curiously, Emily caught herself in mid-sniffle, but managed to take a deep breath to cover it.

"It's just,,," She honestly didn't know.

"Pre-Christmas blues?"

"Year-end blahs?"

"Desperate need for a third child?"

That earned them a bark of laughter that made all four children stir in their sleep.

They all held their breaths until the kids had resettled and the only sounds were the fierce Montana winds struggling vainly to rattle the solid house.

"Not a chance," Emily kept her voice low just in case they weren't fully asleep again. "I don't think Mark would mind, but having your kids late means all sorts of strange things. I'll be sixty before this one graduates from college." She could feel Belle so warm and safe against her side. What would it be like when Belle was a woman grown like Julie or Chelsea and maybe with a child of her own? Out in the world where Emily couldn't protect her?

At Tessa's age, she herself had already had a crush on Peter Matthews—the perfect older boy next door. But he'd married and become President of the United States. She'd gone to West Point and become the first woman of the Night Stalkers. By Julie and Chelsea's age, she'd been flying helicopters on her second tour into war zones with the 101st Airborne.

"Sixty? Shit, you *are* old, sis."

"Go to hell, Chelsea."

"Not gonna happen. I've got you for a big sister, means I've gotta being doing something right."

Emily knew Chelsea had earned a laugh, but she couldn't seem to find it. She lay her head back on the couch and wondered what was wrong with her. Maybe it *was* just the season. Or that Night Stalkers helicopter pilots, unlike most Special Operations Forces, could fly well into their fifties—if they hadn't reproduced. It wasn't some rule that had kept her out. Instead, her own fears for her child's safety had cost her that finely-honed *edge* that made a true Spec Ops pilot. Maybe it was that…

Something was wrong, and she had no idea what.

She heard a soft gasp from Chelsea that made her open her eyes.

And looked up directly into Peter's. Mark and Peter were grinning at her—upside down over the back of the soft, brown-leather couch.

"Surprise, Squirt."

"You're supposed to be in Washington, D.C., Sneaker Boy." Her childhood nickname for the former President of the United States. Except he wasn't anymore. He was the Secretary of State. His nickname was still Sneaker Boy.

She heard a deep, guffaw in the background.

"Hi, Frank."

"Good afternoon, Major Beale," the head of Peter's Secret Service Protection Detail sounded as formal as ever. Yet another reminder of what she'd left behind.

Then she looked over at Mark.

"You seemed kinda down, Emily. So I invited Peter out for Christmas as a surprise. His wife, kid, and maybe a few others will be out next week."

"You're feeling down?" Peter suddenly sounded worried. Just exactly what she didn't need—the Secretary of State and former President flying to Montana in the middle of winter to hover. There'd be no point trying to explain it to Mark; he'd never be convinced he'd over-reacted.

"You're what?" "What's wrong?" Apparently done with the horses, Chelsea's and Julie's husbands chimed in from somewhere out of view.

Emily sat up and looked at her younger sisters. "Don't bother killing me, just take Mark for yourselves, please. Now."

"Do you really change diapers?" Chelsea turned to Mark, who shrugged a yes.

"Dibs," Julie said again.

CHAPTER 2

"Seriously, Em. What's wrong?"

She'd led Peter through the bitter cold out to the horse barn, because no matter what Mark thought, the Secretary of State didn't fly to Montana just because a friend was feeling sad. Though she had to give Mark a few points for noticing how she *was* feeling when she'd barely realized it herself.

She stopped at Chesapeake's stall. The barn was warm with the scent of horse and hay. The light was dim beneath the blowing storm, making it feel almost as cozy as the kitchen—as long as you were wearing a jacket or a horse blanket.

She hadn't had the clarity of mind to remember to grab a treat from the house, but Chelsea kept a bag of carrots in her office and Emily had grabbed one as she walked by.

Breaking off a piece, she palmed it to her horse. The big chestnut mare lipped it off her palm and crunched it down. She leaned her cheek against the horse's and felt her chew.

"Mark's right. You are looking down."

"Which isn't why you're here."

"Well, not all of it, but—"

"Why are you here, Sneaker Boy?"

Peter laughed, then startled when Julie's black-and-white painted horse, Clarence, stuck his head out of his stall to see what was going on and almost knocked Peter over.

Emily gave him a chunk of Chesapeake's carrot as a reward.

"I don't know as I'd have come for either reason separately, but when Mark called to invite me out and…" he shrugged. "It's about Dilya."

She spun to face him, but he only looked concerned, not afraid.

"What about her?" Emily barely managed to keep her voice steady. Dilya was the war-orphan adopted daughter of her best friend Archie and his wife Kee, the first woman to qualify for the Night Stalkers after she herself had. That terrified and starved ten-year-old was now a lovely seventeen-year-old, living in the White House as nanny to the First and Second children.

"She's…" Peter's face showed that he really didn't know as he stumbled to a halt.

"Okay. Not sick. Not in trouble. What?"

Peter finally shrugged. "She reminds me too much of you."

"Of me?" She showed him how to hold some carrot to

feed to Clarence before she fed the greens to Chesapeake. Why on earth would that be?

"Remember when we first met?"

"No. I think I was about three days old. My memory is good, but even I have limits."

"I mean when we re-met."

"You mean when I slammed the head of your Protection Detail onto his ass on the White House's main staircase?" She raised her voice enough to make sure Frank Adams could hear her as he returned from checking that there were no four-legged assassins lurking in the horse barn.

"Are we really back to this, Major? You just gotta keep bringing that up, don't you?"

"It *was* memorable."

Frank grumbled as he moved by to check the other end of the barn.

"Yes," Peter waited until Frank was again out of earshot. "I'd been following your career for some time by then. And I was horrified at the dangers you were going into."

"Because I was a woman."

Peter looked down and scuffed one of his perfect leather shoes at the dirty straw. For all his supposed sophistication, he was still a guy—which meant she'd never understand him.

"That," he admitted, "and because you were my friend. You were the little girl next door who was suddenly flying thirty-million-dollar helicopters straight into harm's way."

"What has this got to do with Dilya?"

193

"You know that girl's nose for trouble?"

"You don't know the half of it." In her first month after they'd rescued her, Dilya had identified two men so intent on revenge that they didn't care if it could start the next World War. Then she'd stowed away on a clandestine insertion deep into Uzbekistan to stop them. A detail that was never included in any action report.

"And I'm guessing I don't want to. But now? I'm getting worried for her, Em."

Emily glanced up at her secure office within the stable. Her Tac Room (short for Tactical) had been built directly over the Tack Room (filled with saddles and bridles). It had been finished with the same, aged wood, so that it didn't stand out at all. Its windows were dark—with special glass that appeared opaque even when lit from within. The only clue from the outside that it was anything special was the very sophisticated lock mounted out of sight from below. From there, at Peter's behest, she'd created the White House Protection Force. The WHPF had proven to be immensely successful, saving the new President's life on three separate occasions and averting any number of other minor disasters.

And despite Emily's best intentions, Dilya had several times ended up far too close to the action for comfort. The last time, nearly being shot down over Canadian soil.

"So, what do you want me to do? Scare her straight?"

She could see Peter's face brighten.

"You know that's not going to happen, don't you?"

And he looked worried again.

"She's an incredibly bright kid. And she's grown up with the elite Night Stalkers company for companions, a sniper mother, a strategic consultant father, and essentially unlimited access to your and now Zachary's White House. You think she was just being cute all those times she 'hung out' in the Oval with you? I guarantee you that Dilya was never an innocent child—at least not since we found her. Watching both your parents be executed right in front of you will do that to a kid."

Peter leaned sadly against the stall door. His idea of casual was a two-piece suit rather than a three-piece under his heavy black wool coat. Clarence snorted in his ear and made him jump away in alarm. Out of carrot, she made a point of scritching the horse's cheek with her fingers until he huffed out a happy sigh.

"If we can't keep her out of trouble, how do we teach her to judge when she's in too deep or at least to cry for help?"

Emily leaned back against Chesapeake's neck. Her childhood friend had been Peter, who was six years older than she was. Julie had been right, Emily knew things because she was out ahead of them…but Belle was two and Tessa was five. That wasn't seventeen. She knew nothing yet about anything after age five. Her only solution had been to treat Dilya as a small adult…one who wasn't so small anymore.

But it was a crucial question. Peter was right, Dilya's well-being depended on it. And she knew just who to ask.

Convincing Peter that there were some things he didn't want to know had proved just as hard as usual, but Emily had practice at it. With Frank's help, she soon had him shooed back over to the main house.

Mounting the stairs to her Tac Room, she keycoded the door, offered her eye for retinal scan, then locked the door behind her.

The one-way glass gave her a long view of the horse stalls, their occupants lazing through the cold winter day, happily napping and munching on hay. Chelsea came into the barn at the far end of the stalls. She waved up as she always did in case Emily was watching, and headed into her own office. As the ranch's horse manager, she was meticulous in the care of her charges and the recent vet's visit to give all of them a checkup had probably left a pile of paperwork.

Emily liked the company when they were both working out here, even if they were isolated in separate offices. Chelsea didn't have the security clearance to ever be inside this room.

Emily had already done her check of the public world news this morning. Now, in her secure space, she flipped through today's briefing documents from the various agencies. No real surprises—hot spots were still hot, but nothing abnormal. She'd be paged if there was a real crisis calling for her attention, but it wasn't the sort of day where that seemed likely. The First and Second families were having their typical White House workdays without travel. Which also meant Dilya would be rattling around the White House.

She tapped in a coded signal and settled in to wait while she read up on that latest internal status reports from NATO.

Her Tac Room assistant, Lauren, had proved herself immensely capable when dealing with military contacts. But the other side of Emily's information network—the one that reached deep into the White House itself—no one knew about except herself. With Lauren honeymooning at Disneyland over the holidays, Emily didn't have to worry about shooing her out to place this call.

"Hello, my dear." Her central screen lit with the face of one of the White House Protection Force's primary assets. Her gray hair framed an ageless face. Sometimes it seemed she'd aged past old crone and gone straight on to wizened. At other times, her face was clear enough that the gray hair was a shock. Today, she simply appeared what she was—a beautiful woman in her seventies (probably).

Behind her ranged the most unusual library in Washington, DC—which was saying something. Emily knew from her one visit there that it wasn't large. Her office felt even smaller because every inch of wall space from floor to ceiling was packed solid with books. Also on display were some of the more clandestine tools of the spy trade, which the shadows hadn't afforded her a chance to study. It was also perhaps the most accurate library on spies and spy craft ever assembled. There were less than a dozen people who knew where it lay—behind the door of Room 043-Mechanical in the White House Residence's deepest subbasement. And the woman in charge had been one of the greatest spies, including undocumented ones, of them all.

A blurred red-and-green glow stood to one side of the camera's view—too close to be clearly seen. A desktop Christmas tree perhaps? What did a master spy's Christmas tree look like? Probably a cone of stacked red-and-green code books used over the last half-century.

"Hello, Miss Watson. How are you today?"

"Oh, I'm good my dear. Very good. Thank you for asking. Is there something amiss that I'm unaware of?"

"Not likely," Emily sometimes wondered if Miss Watson was helping her keep the White House safe or if she was helping Miss Watson.

Miss Watson offered one of her grandmotherly smiles, "I don't know that you've ever made a social call before."

And at Emily's wince, Miss Watson clearly understood that this one wasn't either.

It wasn't that she didn't want to, it was that she never thought to. Not a single one of those fine skills that her mother, one of DC social queens, had struggled to culti-vate in her only offspring had stuck.

"Emily, dear child…"

She almost laughed. She now had two younger "sis-ters" and all of them had children, yet—

"Tell me the reason you called, then we can talk about why you should have called earlier."

Emily tried looking at the books behind Miss Watson. Was there a guide to mindreading tucked away some-where on those shelves? Unsure quite what Miss Watson meant, she described Peter's concerns about Dilya.

"That child was never young. Such potential."

Emily suddenly wasn't sure that Miss Watson's influ-ence on Dilya was a good thing. What little she knew of Miss Watson's exploits told of the immense risks a woman could take in the name of the Cold War. It had been inevitable that Dilya's natural inquisitiveness had brought them together. Unfortunately what happened at the White House was outside of her control. Emily could protect, but she couldn't control.

Instead, her skill had always been in locating and culti-vating exceptional talent. The President's new driver, one of his dog handlers, and others she'd helped put in place kept the President safer far beyond anything the Secret Service would understand—or ever be told about.

The White House Protection Force did *not* include Dilya, and yet she seemed to end up in the center of every problem—even when those problems became life-threatening.

"The girl is so independent. Perhaps too much so."

"Too much?" Emily had always prided herself on her

own independence. It was what had let her succeed in a male world—absolute self-reliance.

"Yes. She knows a great deal more about depending solely on her own judgment than even you, my dear child. Despite your deservedly decorated career. And don't we both know about some of the decorations you can never admit to."

Emily kept her best neutral expression on her face, but Miss Watson merely winked. No one, but *no one* other than the former President and the Joint Chiefs of Staff should know about her medals from black-in-black operations. Even Mark didn't know about those. No more than he'd know that she was technically still on active duty as a consultant.

"Dilya has carefully positioned herself to know more than everyone around her here at the White House," Miss Watson continued blithely. "I even hold a hope that someday she— Well, never mind that now. I believe that you've raised a valid question and I shall give it some thought. It is Christmas soon. Perhaps I shall give her a Christmas gift after all."

Emily considered what that might mean and suddenly wished she hadn't placed this call in the first place. Perhaps she should call Dilya and warn her away from Miss Watson. Actually, she could think of no faster way to drive Dilya directly into the fray. In that, she and Dilya were much alike.

Before Emily could open her mouth to protest or perhaps even try to call Miss Watson off, she continued so smoothly that Emily never managed a word.

"Now, my dear. Let's talk about what's troubling you."

"Nothing's troubling me."

"It isn't age," Miss Watson ignored her fib. "No woman as beautiful as you with two lovely children and such an exceptional husband can doubt that she is in the prime of her life."

She sighed.

"And I must compliment you on the fine job you did helping your husband transition to retired life. You are much better with people than you think you are. You picture yourself so austere and remote, yet people are drawn to you anyway."

Emily opened her mouth to protest, then closed it. She *had* just acquired two younger sisters this morning. Miss Watson couldn't know about them, could she? At least not yet? But she was right, the emotions on their faces had been no lie. Emily had always built team loyalty by being the best—no matter what it cost her. By being the best, she'd attracted the best. Yet it wasn't by outperforming anyone on the team that Julie had asked, *I thought we liked Emily?* And Chelsea had agreed, *We really do.*

"I remember such a time of reflection shortly before I died."

"You…died?"

"Oh yes, dear. Any number of times." She nudged a finger against the Christmas tree that was just a blur on the edge of the screen. It moved, so it wasn't books. Maybe it was better if she didn't know. "It is an easy way to cover your tracks in an on-going operation. But I'm referring to when I let the CIA believe I had died."

"How did they take it?"

"Oh, it was a lovely funeral. I have a star up on their wall, which is quite an honor in my business."

"And they still don't know about you surviving?"

Miss Watson shrugged, "There comes a time in a woman's life where one must move closer to the heart. We aren't men, after all."

Emily felt that was rather obvious.

"You'll want to think about that, child. You are a woman grown. You've fought for the right, and done the duties that a man does. For great achievers like us, struggling within a society not ready for us, we must now come to terms with being...ourselves."

"How did you do it?"

But Miss Watson's ghost of a smile demurred.

How had she done it? From what little Emily knew, Miss Watson might have always been in the White House subbasement. Yet apparently she'd also been a spy in the final years of the Vietnam War and had a Soviet two-star general as a lover. Emily, too, heard things.

She'd first met Miss Watson years before during her brief residence at the White House as the First Lady's personal chef. She'd thought nothing of it at the time— some elderly White House staffer she'd chatted with about the war she was fighting in Afghanistan. In hindsight Emily could see that things had changed for her from that moment. She'd— "Oh, I became *your* weapon."

Miss Watson offered her a slightly surprised expression.

"All those additional black-in-black ops. The toughest missions—"

"—Came to you because of your supreme confidence

and exceptional abilities. Don't try to make me the wizard behind the curtain of your career, Emily. You are tactically an exceptional woman. It is the bigger picture that slips by you. Dilya is beginning to see her own bigger picture, which is why you worry about her—we fear what we don't understand."

"But—"

"Oh, my dear child," Miss Watson was gently shaking her head. "In the later years, you are still *yourself*. But the challenges are new. You must learn who you, yourself are. Rediscover or, if that fails, discover for the first time, the amazing woman you are."

"That's your advice?"

"The voice of experience."

Emily couldn't help but remember Julie leaning forward just this morning, *She knows things. I vote that we keep her.*

Man oh man, did she ever have them fooled.

"What did you—"

"Oh no, child. It would be cheating to tell. Besides, Dilya is far more my daughter than you are—at least in how she thinks. You must discover your own woman."

"Why doesn't that feel helpful?"

"Because you're still thinking as if you live in a man's world, challenging the status quo." Then Miss Watson shook herself lightly, glanced at her bookshelves somewhere out of sight, and suddenly appeared much older.

"Miss Watson, are you—"

"It is time I sent for Dilya."

"Miss Watson?" Emily could think of nothing else to say.

"Go see your family, dear." Then she was gone.

Emily sat in her small Tac Room and looked at blank screen, she tried not to feel sadder than before the call. Did the poor woman even have any family? Did she even have someone to spend Christmas with? Not that Emily knew of, and yet here she was dumping her own doubts upon Miss Watson.

She knew she could trust Dilya to Miss Watson's care and she'd hear soon enough what had happened. Emily had forgotten how much she liked Miss Watson and promised herself that her next call would be strictly social. Or when she needed a break from the Montana winter, she'd visit her parents in DC and arrange to drop in on the White House subbasement personally.

As for herself, none of it felt like a solution to anything.

"What are you up to, babe?" Mark slid down on the couch beside her. He flipped up the edge of the big Cheyenne weaving she'd thrown over herself hours before while she'd watched the fire burn. There were only a few embers left, dying from lack of tending.

"What time is it?"

"Way early, but I missed you in bed." He pulled her into his arms and kissed her on the temple.

A week had passed and she was no closer to understanding any of Miss Watson's life lessons. Now she was out of time and simply had to shake it off.

Later today the ranch house would become much more lively. Vice President Daniel Darlington and his family had decided to fly out for Christmas along with Peter's wife and child. The local ranchers' potluck was going to get a big surprise tonight—for security's sake, no one would be warned ahead of time. Of course surprises were fair on both sides of the coin—she also hadn't forewarned the Secret Service just how many rifles would arrive tonight, hanging in the back windows of Montana pickup trucks.

The girls' pillow igloo fort would have to come down —or it should. Knowing she'd lose that battle, she decided to leave well enough alone. Julie's husband Nathan and Mark's mom Ama would be awake soon and the three of them were planning to cook throughout the day. All week, Peter had practically taken over her secure Tac Room in the barn, doing Secretary of State things, so at least he'd been out from underfoot.

With the ease of long practice, Mark had eased her into his lap with her barely noticing until her head lay on his shoulder and his hand cradled her behind underneath the warm blanket.

"This isn't like you, Emily. Got me worried some." She'd always enjoyed feeling the deep rumble in his chest when he spoke.

"That makes two of us."

"You missing the action?"

She shook her head. At first the adrenaline-junkie withdrawal had been hard, but she'd expected that. Besides, she hadn't gone straight from Spec Ops to civilian—the years flying to wildfire and her occasional calls to consult had eased the transition.

"Sick of the cooking?"

No. She loved that. Mark's mother Ama had run the kitchen for over a decade, but cooked much less now. Nathan, a world-class chef who'd stumbled into love with Julie, had taken over the kitchen with such zeal that Emily could come play whenever the mood struck her, but she didn't have to worry when it didn't.

"Nothing about the kids?"

"I couldn't love Belle and Tessa more if they were part of me."

"They *were* part of you."

"Exactly my point."

As if on cue, the two girls appeared, still rubbing their eyes sleepily. In moments, they were all curled up together under the warm blanket. It was awkward, a little uncomfortable, and amazingly perfect.

"Not…us?" Mark whispered against her ear once the girls were settled. They were huddled under the blanket, mostly on her lap, whispering back and forth.

In answer, she managed to twist around enough to kiss Mark. He made it as thorough and perfect as their very first kiss—and she felt no desire to smash his face into an aircraft carrier's table as she'd done the first time.

"Then what?" Mark asked as she once more lay her head upon his shoulder and tightened her arm around Tessa's waist earning a happy giggle from beneath the big quilt.

For the life of her, she hadn't a clue.

CHAPTER 5

The mayhem had started even sooner than she'd anticipated.

Belle and Tessa, finally coming wide awake under the blanket, had found their father's one ticklish spot and completely undone him. To escape, he'd finally fallen off the couch. Turning it into a roll, he regained his feet and moved over to stoke the fire. The girls knew about not interfering around the flames. By the time she and the girls were dressed, Ama had breakfast on the table. Nathan was eating as he worked, assembling the ingredients for Emily's dry rub on the massive roast they'd planned for the potluck.

Second Lady Alice had arrived with their newborn, and Peter's wife Geneviève brought their little girl. At four, she had all the poise and elegance that her mother embodied and Emily's own daughters completely lacked. Belle and Tessa practically transcended on the spot with the additional playmate. She didn't know if she hoped her girls rubbed off on Adele Gloria—simply to harass Peter

—or perhaps the other way round and her own girls might become more comprehensible to her. Either way, kid heaven had taken over much of the floor space in front of the fireplace with Mark often in the fray.

Her mood kept lifting through the day.

She'd never thought of herself as a particularly social or even approachable woman, but there were only so many welcoming hugs and joyous smiles that could be aimed her way before that belief became undeniably foolish.

Thankfully, the storm blew out and all that was left were achingly clear starlit skies and bitter cold. But Montanan ranchers had never yet been stopped by mere cold and soon the house was packed. The local ranchers soon shed their awe of the Washington elite—helped in part by all of the children in their pre-Christmas excitement. As more local children had arrived, they'd strained Tessa's and Belle's "dress up" wardrobe to the limit, but Christmas fairies and elves had abounded.

The big afternoon puppy-pile nap on the kitchen's couch had averted most of the exhaustion meltdowns.

And somehow, through the whole thing, the Christmas igloo fort had survived—no mere "tent" could have made it through the constant stream of children in and out of it. Of all the adults, only Mark had been allowed admittance.

As the evening wound down and the ranchers drifted back home through the chill darkness, the family and Washington guests slowly gathered once more in the kitchen. Chairs and benches were dragged over until everyone was packed in close to the fireplace. Hot cocoa, laced with brandy for the grownups, was served all around.

Emily could only look around the circle in wonder. Julie and Chelsea sat nearby with their husbands and babies. Her childhood friend Peter and his lovely Geneviève sat with her friend Vice President Daniel and his cheery wife. All around the room, there wasn't a person here whose life she hadn't touched, and who hadn't touched hers.

How had she not known this? Why was she just seeing it now?

These were her friends. Her family. Just as surely as the action teams of the Night Stalkers 5th Battalion D Company and the firefighters of Mount Hood Aviation had been her family.

She…belonged.

Is this what Miss Watson had been talking about? That somehow, this was her "woman's" role after having lived in the "man's" world for so many years?

Maybe it was. Maybe—

"I think it's time, girls," Mark called, loudly enough to silence all of the conversations.

With a squeal of delight, they launched to their feet in a mad swirl of excitement and fairy wings. Adele Gloria—Peter's and Geneviève's daughter had devolved only a little under Tessa's influence and Tessa had settled (a little) —was rapidly recruited and the three kids disappeared into the Christmas igloo fort.

"Now it's your turn, honey," Mark rose and held out his hand to her.

Emily was terribly conscious that everyone was

watching her as she rose to her feet. She should have gone and locked herself in her Tac Room—nobody would dare to disturb her there. Then she certainly wouldn't be the center of attention.

Once she was on her feet, Mark knelt before her, something he hadn't even done while proposing. What was he—

"Up," he patted his shoulder.

"What?"

He hooked one of her knees and dragged it over his shoulder. "Climb aboard, Emily."

"No. I—" she resisted his attempt to grab her other leg.

"Here, Mommy," Belle came out of the igloo and handed her a package wrapped in Christmas paper before racing back in.

Mark took advantage of her momentary distraction and got her astride his shoulders. Then he stood quickly before she could escape. He faced the Christmas igloo and called out.

"Ready, girls?"

A high chorus of "Yes!" was their answer as she hung onto Mark's forehead with one hand and the wrapped present with the other.

"Go!" Mark roared out like commanding a fleet of weapon-laden helicopters into battle.

The igloo wavered as if hit from the inside. Then it wavered again.

The assembled crowd was absolutely silent in anticipation.

Another impact and one pillow fell off the top of the wall.

Then there was a shout of little girls joining forces in some supreme effort. The three of them, with their arms locked together, burst clean through the side of the pillow igloo, which fell and scattered in every direction.

Emily joined in everyone's gasp of wonder.

The larch tree, that had stood so long in hiding, was revealed. It had been decorated with hand-made ornaments, lights, popcorn-and-cranberry strings, and everything else that little girls and her husband could think of. People were pulling aside the tumbled pillows until a great mound of them had been piled up behind the couch and the tree stood fully revealed.

"It's beautiful," she barely managed a whisper but somehow Mark heard it through all of the applause and general chatter.

"Not finished yet."

"No, it's perfect."

But he stepped up to the tree, giving her the feeling that she was floating along in a helicopter once more. She considered tugging on his ears to see if they acted like rudder controls, or maybe a cyclic to get her down from here. But his big hands were clamped over her thighs, pinning her in place.

"Emily, open your present."

At a loss for what else to do, she unwrapped it as she teetered high in the air. And discovered a golden star.

The bare top of the larch, the only part of the tree that had ever shown above the pillow igloo, was right at eye level. By reaching out as far as she dared, she was just able to slip it onto the top of the tree.

A fresh round of cheers and applause broke out as

Mark stepped back and helped her down to the pine floor. The tree was glorious with its wild decorations and brightly colored lights set off by the golden warmth of the fire's flickering glow.

With Mark's arm around her waist, and the girls' hanging on to either side, they all admired the tree.

Or at least Mark and the girls did.

Emily instead heard the joy and the laughter of her friends gathered around her. So many. So true.

"You're my star," Mark whispered—absolutely the romantic one in their relationship.

This right here, this moment was who she *truly* was.

And Emily could feel that gift all the way to her heart.

And don't miss the companion story: Dilya's Christmas Challenge, a White House Protection Force story.

DILYA'S CHRISTMAS CHALLENGE (EXCERPT)

DON'T MISS THIS WONDERFUL COMPANION STORY TO EMILY'S CHRISTMAS

Teenager Dilya Stevenson's *life at the White House is like no one else's. As the First Family's nanny and dog walker, her duties are sometimes light and always enjoyable. Which leaves her plenty of time to keep her eyes and ears open behind the scenes. Facing danger as a child, and even death has taught her to be a loner—too much so her elders fear.*

Retired spy Miss Watson *takes pride in trusting no one. But she keeps a weather eye on Dilya from her secret library in the White House's deepest basement. Both she and Major Emily Beale, an old friend, wish to save the girl from following in either of their footsteps. Little knowing that all their lives will be impacted, they set Dilya's Christmas Challenge.*

DILYA'S CHRISTMAS CHALLENGE
(EXCERPT)

Miss Watson had considered painting a giant spider web on her door. If it wouldn't draw undue attention, she well might have. Room 043-Mechanical in the White House Residence's lowest subbasement had nothing mechanical in it, at least nothing that a building engineer would ever care about. Good cover because the best cover was a bland one.

Her small desk had once belonged to Assistant Secretary of the Treasury, Harry Dexter White, who had run the Silvermaster spy ring for the Soviet Union for years. Her walls were packed with every biography or interview transcript from a spy going back to the early days of the American colonies. The rubbish about The Craft that consumed so much of the CIA's libraries—written by analysts and others even less informed—were not to be found within her four walls. She also kept a number of the more gruesome tools of the trade on display to remind her of just what horrors the human psyche was capable.

But even at her age, a woman wasn't supposed to feel

like Moriarty—Sherlock Holmes' greatest opponent—curled "motionless, like a spider in the centre of its web, but that web has a thousand radiations, and he knows well every quiver of each of them."

She rarely left her office anymore, instead listening only to the information that flowed into her domain rather than gathering it. She allowed only a few bits, a very precious few, to flow back out. Maybe she'd paint the spider web in blacklight or some other ink that wouldn't show. But she'd know was there.

It always surprised her when a thread was activated that she hadn't anticipated. When the computer beeped she dropped a stitch in her knitting in surprise—a nice bit of double-sided colorwork scarf recalling a long ago sunset along the shore of the Black Sea.

Assumptions are dangerous, she reminded herself.

She forced herself to pick up the stitch and count to make sure that everything was put to rights before she answered.

"Hello, my dear." Her screen lit to reveal one of her favorite people. Major Emily Beale (retired—at least according to most official records) had a mind that worked so differently from her own. For that reason if no other, Emily would have been very useful to her. But as a force of nature in her own right, the immensely skilled and well-connected woman brought far more assets than most could muster.

However, she should have known a call was coming. It wasn't unusual for Emily to call from her Montana ranch, but it was strange that she herself had no inkling of what the topic might be.

"Hello, Miss Watson. How are you today?"

"Oh, I'm good my dear. Very good. Thank you for asking. Is there something amiss that I'm unaware of?"

"Not likely."

Miss Watson couldn't quite resist smiling at the compliment. "I don't know that you've ever made a social call before."

Emily's grimace communicated a great deal. It wasn't social, which was disappointing. But she saw in how Emily's eyes shifted to the side, beyond the breadth of the screen she'd be using, that Emily wished it had been. She was such a sweet woman.

"Emily, dear child…" Miss Watson merely said it to herself, but saw Emily react much more strongly than expected.

A laugh?

A hysterical one?

Major Emily Beale was not the sort given to hysterics.

"Tell me the reason you called, then we can talk about why you should have called earlier."

Emily nodded, "I'm worried about Dilya. She keeps placing herself at risk. I don't want her to create a situation that's over her head when she's too young to know what she's doing."

"That child was never young. Such potential." She regretted the last as soon as she said it aloud. She could see the sudden wariness in Emily's eyes—so protective of the teen, despite the girl being adopted not by her but by one of her teammates. That protectiveness was one of Emily's great strengths. Her own instincts were far more honed to self-preservation.

Dilya, as a seventeen-year-old war orphan, was much the same. She'd been afforded the best training imaginable: her deep involvement with the fighting elements of the Night Stalkers 5th Battalion D Company, who had rescued her originally. Her placement in the White House as a nanny and then the dog minder for the First Dog had placed her in the way of exceptional information. Her skills at passing through a room unremarked were truly exceptional. It definitely reminded Miss Watson of her own, long ago youth.

And most importantly, Dilya possessed the sharp mind to go with it.

That girl's mind... Yet Emily had a point.

"The girl is so independent. Perhaps too much so." How different would her own past be if she had learned to rely upon others? Even occasionally?

"Too much?" And there was Emily's limitation. Her definition of success was the survival of her team and the destruction of her target. She was terribly linear. Independence was a lesson that Emily only thought she had learned. She had been embedded in teams her entire life.

"Yes. She knows a great deal more about depending solely on her own judgment than even you, my dear child. Despite your deservedly decorated career. And don't we both know about some of the decorations you can never admit to."

Emily's bland expression would be a sufficient denial —to anyone who hadn't spent a lifetime surviving by studying human body language. She almost considered pointing out how easy she was to read for a professional, but decided that there were some things Emily would be happier never knowing.

Dilya's strength was in her covert gathering of knowledge. But oh, the price that was paid for such a gift. Miss Watson both envied and pitied the girl.

"Dilya has carefully positioned herself to know more than everyone around her," Miss Watson continued, more to herself than Emily. "I even hold a hope that someday she—"

Not yet. She didn't dare think that far ahead. Hope often hurt as much as it helped.

"Well, never mind that now. I believe that you've raised a valid question and I shall give it some thought. It is Christmas soon. Perhaps I shall give her a Christmas gift."

———

Keep reading at fine retailers everywhere:
Dilya's Christmas Challenge
...and please leave a review. Thanks!

BIG SKY DOG WHISPERER

This title fits nicely here.

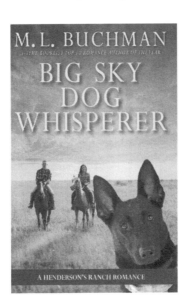

Two military dog handlers retired: one to New York, one to Montana's Big Sky. Now their dogs must bring them together.

*Petty Officer Jodie Jaffe brought her war dog home after they
were both blown up on patrol. She's fine, honest, but her dog is
shattered with PTSD.*

*SEAL Team 6 handler Stan Corman left his dog's ashes and a
part of himself overseas. For three years he's been training a
new litter. Knowing he'll never be whole again, he hopes his
dogs can save lives even if he no longer can.*

*But when Jodie brings her damaged dog to the ranch, Stan faces
far more than he counted on...or knows how to handle.*

*[Can be read stand-alone or in series. A complete happy-ever-
after with no cliffhangers. Originally published as #8 in the
series because of short stories that are now collected together in
a final volume.]*

Grab it now at fine retailers everywhere:
Big Sky Dog Whisperer

AFTERWORD

I was done with Henderson's Ranch, but it wasn't quite done with me. I had told the stories of the founding of a unique ranch and lifestyle in the stark and remarkable Front Range of Montana.

But Henderson's Ranch wasn't done with me. I should have known that, simply from the ties back to the White House Protection Force. But that wasn't where the story went next.

Instead, my ShadowForce: PSI team took a trip there for *At the Quietest Word.* And then the Henderson's Ranch team came to ShadowForce's rescue in *At the Clearest Sensation.*

Done yet?

Nope. Dilya—remember all the way back to Night Stalkers #2, *I Own the Dawn*—was not to be so lightly dismissed. She had adventure in and out of numerous series, including key roles throughout The Night Stalkers Holidays and White House Protection Force series.

Well, she's grown now, a skilled dog handler, and a

professional snoop. Coming soon, she'll be returning to Henderson's Ranch but with her own series in tow, Dilya's Dog Force—launching in new directions that, as of this writing, only Dilya knows.

If you enjoyed this book,
please consider leaving a review.
They really help.

Keep reading for an exciting excerpt from:
Off the Leash

OFF THE LEASH (EXCERPT)

IF YOU ENJOYED THIS, YOU'LL LOVE THE
WHITE HOUSE PROTECTION FORCE SERIES

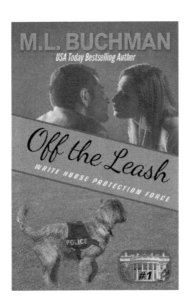

"You're joking."

"Nope. That's his name. And he's yours now."

Sergeant Linda Hamlin wondered quite what it would take to wipe that smile off Lieutenant Jurgen's face. A 120mm round from an M1A1 Abrams Main Battle Tank came to mind.

The kennel master of the US Secret Service's Canine Team was clearly a misogynistic jerk from the top of his polished head to the bottoms of his equally polished boots. She wondered if the shoelaces were polished as well.

Then she looked over at the poor dog sitting hopefully on the concrete kennel floor. His stall had a dog bed three times his size and a water bowl deep enough for him to bathe in. No toys, because toys always came from the handler as a reward. He offered her a sad sigh and a liquid doggy gaze. The kennel even smelled wrong, more of sanitizer than dog. The walls seemed to echo with each bark down the long line of kennels housing the candidate hopefuls for the next addition to the Secret Service's team.

Thor—really?—was a brindle-colored mutt, part who-knew and part no-one-cared. He looked like a cross between an oversized, long-haired schnauzer and a dust mop that someone had spilled dark gray paint on. After mixing in streaks of tawny brown, they'd left one white paw just to make him all the more laughable.

And of course Lieutenant Jerk Jurgen would assign Thor to the first woman on the USSS K-9 team.

Unable to resist, she leaned over far enough to scruff the dog's ears. He was the physical opposite of the sleek and powerful Malinois MWDs—military war dogs—that she'd been handling for the 75th Rangers for the last five years. They twitched with eagerness and nerves. A good MWD was seventy pounds of pure drive—every damn second of the day. If the mild-mannered Thor weighed thirty pounds, she'd be surprised. And he looked like a little girl's best friend who should have a pink bow on his collar.

Jurgen was clearly ex-Marine and would have no respect for the Army. Of course, having been in the Army's Special Operations Forces, she knew better than to respect a Marine.

"We won't let any old swabbie bother us, will we?"

Jurgen snarled—definitely Marine Corps. Swabbie was slang for a Navy sailor and a Marine always took offense at being lumped in with them no matter how much they belonged. Of course the swabbies took offense at having the Marines lumped with *them*. Too bad there weren't any Navy around so that she could get two for the price of one. Jurgen wouldn't be her boss, so appeasing him wasn't high on her to-do list.

At least she wouldn't need any of the protective bite gear working with Thor. With his stature, he was an explosives detection dog without also being an attack one.

"Where was he trained?" She stood back up to face the beast.

"Private outfit in Montana—some place called Henderson's Ranch. Didn't make their MWD program," his scoff said exactly what he thought the likelihood of any dog outfit in Montana being worthwhile. "They wanted us to try the little runt out."

She'd never heard of a training program in Montana. MWDs all came out of Lackland Air Force Base training. The Secret Service mostly trained their own and they all came from Vohne Liche Kennels in Indiana. Unless… Special Operations Forces dogs were trained by private contractors. She'd worked beside a Delta Force dog for a single month—he'd been incredible.

"Is he trained in English or German?" Most American MWDs were trained in German so that there was no confusion in case a command word happened to be part of a spoken sentence. It also made it harder for any random person on the battlefield to shout something that would confuse the dog.

"German according to his paperwork, but he won't listen to me much in either language."

Might as well give the diminutive Thor a few basic tests. A snap of her fingers and a slap on her thigh had the dog dropping into a smart "heel" position. No need to call out *Fuss—by my foot.*

"Pass auf!" Guard! She made a pistol with her thumb and forefinger and aimed it at Jurgen as she grabbed her forearm with her other hand—the military hand sign for enemy.

The little dog snarled at Jurgen sharply enough to have him backing out of the kennel. "Goddamn it!"

"Ruhig." Quiet. Thor maintained his fierce posture but dropped the snarl.

"Gute Hund." Good dog, Linda countered the command.

Thor looked up at her and wagged his tail happily. She tossed him a doggie treat, which he caught midair and crunched happily.

She didn't bother looking up at Jurgen as she knelt once more to check over the little dog. His scruffy fur was so soft that it tickled. Good strength in the jaw, enough to show he'd had bite training despite his size—perfect if she ever needed to take down a three-foot-tall terrorist. Legs said he was a jumper.

"Take your time, Hamlin. I've got nothing else to do with the rest of my goddamn day except babysit you and this mutt."

"Is the course set?"

"Sure. Take him out," Jurgen's snarl sounded almost as nasty as Thor's before he stalked off.

She stood and slapped a hand on her opposite shoulder.

Thor sprang aloft as if he was attached to springs and she caught him easily. He'd cleared well over double his own height. Definitely trained...and far easier to catch than seventy pounds of hyperactive Malinois.

She plopped him back down on the ground. On lead

or off? She'd give him the benefit of the doubt and try off first to see what happened.

Linda zipped up her brand-new USSS jacket against the cold and led the way out of the kennel into the hard sunlight of the January morning. Snow had brushed the higher hills around the USSS James J. Rowley Training Center—which this close to Washington, DC, wasn't saying much—but was melting quickly. Scents wouldn't carry as well on the cool air, making it more of a challenge for Thor to locate the explosives. She didn't know where they were either. The course was a test for handler as well as dog.

Jurgen would be up in the observer turret looking for any excuse to mark down his newest team. Perhaps teasing him about being just a Marine hadn't been her best tactical choice. She sighed. At least she was consistent —she'd always been good at finding ways to piss people off before she could stop herself and consider the wisdom of doing so.

This test was the culmination of a crazy three months, so she'd forgive herself this time—something she also wasn't very good at.

In October she'd been out of the Army and unsure what to do next. Tucked in the packet with her DD 214 honorable discharge form had been a flyer on career opportunities with the US Secret Service dog team: *Be all your dog can be!* No one else being released from Fort Benning that day had received any kind of a job flyer at all that she'd seen, so she kept quiet about it.

She had to pass through DC on her way back to Vermont—her parent's place. Burlington would work for, honestly, not very long at all, but she lacked anywhere else to go after a decade of service. So, she'd stopped off in DC to see what was up with that job flyer. Five interviews and three months to complete a standard six-month training course later—which was mostly a cakewalk after fighting with the US Rangers—she was on-board and this chill January day was her first chance with a dog. First chance to prove that she still had it. First chance to prove that she hadn't made a mistake in deciding that she'd seen enough bloodshed and war zones for one lifetime and leaving the Army.

The Start Here sign made it obvious where to begin, but she didn't dare hesitate to take in her surroundings past a quick glimpse. Jurgen's score would count a great deal toward where she and Thor were assigned in the future. Mostly likely on some field prep team, clearing the way for presidential visits.

As usual, hindsight informed her that harassing the lieutenant hadn't been an optimal strategy. A hindsight that had served her equally poorly with regular Army commanders before she'd finally hooked up with the Rangers—kowtowing to officers had never been one of her strengths.

Thankfully, the Special Operations Forces hadn't given a damn about anything except performance and *that* she could always deliver, since the day she'd been named the team captain for both soccer and volleyball. She was never popular, but both teams had made all-state her last two years in school.

The canine training course at James J. Rowley was a two-acre lot. A hard-packed path of tramped-down dirt led through the brown grass. It followed a predictable pattern from the gate to a junker car, over to tool shed, then a truck, and so on into a compressed version of an intersection in a small town. Beyond it ran an urban street of gray clapboard two- and three-story buildings and an eight-story office tower, all without windows. Clearly a playground for Secret Service training teams.

Her target was the town, so she blocked the city street out of her mind. Focus on the problem: two roads, twenty storefronts, six houses, vehicles, pedestrians.

It might look normal...normalish with its missing windows and no movement. It would be anything but. Stocked with fake IEDs, a bombmaker's stash, suicide cars, weapons caches, and dozens of other traps, all waiting for her and Thor to find. He had to be sensitive to hundreds of scents and it was her job to guide him so that he didn't miss the opportunity to find and evaluate each one.

There would be easy scents, from fertilizer and diesel fuel used so destructively in the 1995 Oklahoma City bombing, to almost as obvious TNT to the very difficult to detect C-4 plastic explosive.

Mannequins on the street carried grocery bags and briefcases. Some held fresh meat, a powerful smell demanding any dog's attention, but would count as a false lead if they went for it. On the job, an explosives detection dog wasn't supposed to care about anything except explosives. Other mannequins were wrapped in suicide vests loaded with Semtex or wearing knapsacks filled with package bombs made from Russian PVV-5A.

She spotted Jurgen stepping into a glassed-in observer

turret atop the corner drugstore. Someone else was already there and watching.

She looked down once more at the ridiculous little dog and could only hope for the best.

"Thor?"

He looked up at her.

She pointed to the left, away from the beaten path.

"*Such!*" Find.

Thor sniffed left, then right. Then he headed forward quickly in the direction she pointed.

Clive Andrews sat in the second-story window at the corner of Main and First, the only two streets in town. Downstairs was a drugstore all rigged to explode, except there were no triggers and there was barely enough explosive to blow up a candy box.

Not that he'd know, but that's what Lieutenant Jurgen had promised him.

It didn't really matter if it was rigged to blow for real, because when Miss Watson—never Ms. or Mrs.—asked for a "favor," you did it. At least he did. Actually, he had yet to meet anyone else who knew her. Not that he'd asked around. She wasn't the sort of person one talked about with strangers, or even close friends. He'd bet even if they did, it would be in whispers. That's just what she was like.

So he'd traveled across town from the White House and into Maryland on a cold winter's morning, barely past a sunrise that did nothing to warm the day. Now he sat in an unheated glass icebox and watched a new officer run a test course he didn't begin to understand.

———————

Keep reading at fine retailers everywhere:
Off the Leash
...and please leave a review. Thanks!

ABOUT THE AUTHOR

USA Today and Amazon #1 Bestseller M. L. "Matt" Buchman began writing on a flight from Japan to ride his bicycle across the Australian Outback. Just part of a solo around-the-world trip that ultimately launched his writing career.

From the very beginning, his powerful female heroines insisted on putting character first, *then* a great adventure. He's since written over 70 action-adventure thrillers and military romantic suspense novels. And just for the fun of it: 100 short stories, and a fast-growing pile of read-by-author audiobooks.

Booklist says: "3X Top 10 of the Year." PW says: "Tom Clancy fans open to a strong female lead will clamor for more." His fans say: "I want more now...of everything." That his characters are even more insistent than his fans is a hoot.

As a 30-year project manager with a geophysics degree who has designed and built houses, flown and jumped out of planes, and solo-sailed a 50' ketch, he is awed by what is possible. More at: www.mlbuchman.com.

Other works by M. L. Buchman: *(* - also in audio)*

Action-Adventure Thrillers

Dead Chef
One Chef!
Two Chef!

Miranda Chase
Drone*
Thunderbolt*
Condor*
Ghostrider*
Raider*
Chinook*
Havoc*
White Top*
Start the Chase*

Science Fiction / Fantasy

Deities Anonymous
Cookbook from Hell: Reheated
Saviors 101

Single Titles
Monk's Maze
the Me and Elsie Chronicles

Contemporary Romance

Eagle Cove
Return to Eagle Cove
Recipe for Eagle Cove
Longing for Eagle Cove
Keepsake for Eagle Cove

Love Abroad
Heart of the Cotswolds: England
Path of Love: Cinque Terre, Italy

Where Dreams
Where Dreams are Born
Where Dreams Reside
Where Dreams Are of Christmas*
Where Dreams Unfold
Where Dreams Are Written
Where Dreams Continue

Non-Fiction

Strategies for Success
Managing Your Inner Artist/Writer
Estate Planning for Authors*
Character Voice
Narrate and Record Your Own
Audiobook*

Short Story Series by M. L. Buchman:

Action-Adventure Thrillers

Dead Chef

Miranda Chase Origin Stories

Romantic Suspense

Antarctic Ice Fliers

US Coast Guard

Contemporary Romance

Eagle Cove

Other

Deities Anonymous (fantasy)

Single Titles

The Emily Beale Universe
(military romantic suspense)

The Night Stalkers
MAIN FLIGHT
The Night Is Mine
I Own the Dawn
Wait Until Dark
Take Over at Midnight
Light Up the Night
Bring On the Dusk
By Break of Day
Target of the Heart
Target Lock on Love
Target of Mine
Target of One's Own
NIGHT STALKER HOLIDAYS
*Daniel's Christmas**
*Frank's Independence Day**
*Peter's Christmas**
Christmas at Steel Beach
*Zachary's Christmas**
*Roy's Independence Day**
*Damien's Christmas**
Christmas at Peleliu Cove

Henderson's Ranch
*Nathan's Big Sky**
*Big Sky, Loyal Heart**
*Big Sky Dog Whisperer**
*Tales of Henderson's Ranch**

Shadow Force: Psi
*At the Slightest Sound**
*At the Quietest Word**
*At the Merest Glance**
*At the Clearest Sensation**

Dilya's Dog Force
(formerly:
White House Protection Force)
*Off the Leash**
*On Your Mark**
*In the Weeds**

Firehawks
Pure Heat
Full Blaze
*Hot Point**
*Flash of Fire**
Wild Fire
SMOKEJUMPERS
*Wildfire at Dawn**
*Wildfire at Larch Creek**
*Wildfire on the Skagit**

Delta Force
*Target Engaged**
*Heart Strike**
*Wild Justice**
*Midnight Trust**

Emily Beale Universe Short Story Series
The Night Stalkers
The Night Stalkers Stories
The Night Stalkers CSAR
The Night Stalkers Wedding Stories
The Future Night Stalkers

Delta Force
Th Delta Force Shooters
The Delta Force Warriors

Firehawks
The Firehawks Lookouts
The Firehawks Hotshots
The Firebirds

Dilya's Dog Force
Stories

Future Night Stalkers
Stories (Science Fiction)

The Emily Beale Universe
Reading Order Road Map

any series and any novel may be read stand-alone
(all have a complete heartwarming happy ever after)

* *Formerly*: White House Protection Force
For more information and alternate reading orders, please visit:
www.mlbuchman.com/reading-order

Printed in Great Britain
by Amazon